Jekyll Point

THE WAY BACK

A NOVEL BY

TRICIA ANDREASSEN

Copyright 2024
Tricia Andreassen
Creative Life Publishing

ACKNOWLEDGMENT

I first started coming to Jekyll over 14 years ago for "mom and me trips" with our son, Jordan. These were special bonding times which led to us going as a family for vacations as well as second honeymoon trips for me and Kurt.

I also came to the island by myself to lose myself in this story and connect with these special characters that became close to my heart. Over the years I have developed close friendships that are like second family. This is why I love Jekyll Island. The people here are filled with love, faith, hope and compassion. I would like to thank all my friends along the way that have encouraged me in the writing of this book.

Special thanks to Captain Adam, Jamie Sanders and Captain Phillip of Jekyll Island Dolphin Tours as I have literally lost count at how many times I have been on your boat. Thank you, Jamie, for all the insights on the nature, ecosystems, and behavioral aspects of dolphins.

A heartfelt of gratitude to the Jekyll Island Club Hotel for your incredible service and hospitality on the times I have stayed with you. Thank you, Jekyll Island Art Association, for sharing your art with me and allowing me to be featured as an Artist and Author with your amazing organization. Lewis Baker, and the Friends of Jekyll Island Group, I greatly appreciate you as you all have become friends over these years.

And most of all to my husband Kurt and son Jordan who always support and believe in me. Thank you beyond measure. I dedicate this series to you.

Tricia

CHAPTER 1

ERIN

Maybe I was numb. My throat felt closed, like the emotions were stuck in my windpipe. *What am I doing here?* Nothing within me answered back. Complete silence. Nothing but the sound of waves crashing upon the hardened sand.

I lost myself in the view. The sunset gave a mix of pinks and purples with an extended yellow path on the water. I imagined walking out to the water's edge and stepping on that reflection like it was a trail leading somewhere where everything was perfect. A place with no problems or pain. I would know where to go. I would just step into the light and follow it to wherever it took me.

In just a matter of moments my entire world had crumbled. Up to now, I thought my life was planned out. Until I found Thom in bed with her.

I didn't even want to say her name in my mind. A husband's betrayal was bad enough but with your closest friend? The one who knew all your fears? The one you told your secrets to? The one who believed in your dreams even when you doubted them? The one person who was supposed to be your biggest fan, no matter what? In 48 short hours I had lost the entire support structure I had come to rely on. Knowing what my husband did was bad enough, but the double betrayal made bile rise in the back of my throat.

I swallowed and watched the sky transform into the grayness of the night. Sure, the last couple of years have been tough. Maybe I should have been more cognizant of the stress it was having on our marriage. I guess I was not the fun, carefree girl he married. My Dad's death and my miscarriage at 14 weeks changed something in me on a core level. The miscarriage knocked the wind out of me. To think everything is okay with your pregnancy, only to find out on the sonogram table that the life inside you had died. It felt like the ultimate loss.

During all this, I thought Laura had understood. Yeah, she understood all right. She showed her understanding by taking my husband to bed. Devastation and hopelessness took hold of me, like a root growing into a pipe drain, cutting off the flow of water.

It was getting dark. I needed to get back before I couldn't see my grooved trail in the grassy path. I shook the sand off my towel and threw it into my backpack. Tossing it over my shoulder, I headed back to the rented beach house. Thank God I had Jekyll Island. Jekyll felt reliable to me. For the past five years, it always brought the same quiet peacefulness and slower pace compared to my life back in Charlotte. I found solitude and renewed energy on my previous visits here. I wondered if I could do it this time. This time was different; vastly different.

Thom had only come here once and even then; his phone was glued to his ear most of the time. He was always too busy with work. I preferred coming here by myself. This was a place to disconnect from the stresses of life and reconnect with myself. I loved the undeveloped stretches of sandy beach. Here on the island, I could experience the sunrise over the ocean in the morning and in the evening the sunset over the covered marshes and creeks running into the sound. I could take in a deep breath and smell the salty aroma that felt therapeutic. I could see and hear the gentle lapping of the waves against the shore. It was an overall feeling of rebirth. But what brought me back time and again were my dolphins. Sure, the dolphins weren't really mine. They didn't belong to anyone but to themselves. No wonder they seemed so free to me.

Each trip I always parked my car next to the soccer complex on the island and headed right to Jekyll Point. It was where the Atlantic Ocean merged into the creeks feeding into the sound, like two souls coming together in lovemaking to bring energy into creation. Of all my island explorations I found this was the favored location for sea turtles to come in to lay their eggs. Often on my walks I would come across horseshoe crabs and birds playing chase with the waves. It was like watching children on a playground. A true nature's playground: it also brought my dolphins to me.

For as long as I could remember, I had this crazy belief that if I asked a question or needed insight on some cosmic answer, I could go to the beach and if I saw a dolphin, it would give me the answer. I couldn't explain it. It was like the dolphins could read my mind and answer questions that I had no clear answer to. Jekyll Island was a world of possibilities and new beginnings.

That's why I came here. With all the mess going on in my life I needed this more than ever. Even more than after my dad's death and my miscarriage. Coming here felt like a second home. It was like my soul belonged here. Life just felt easier.

That's why I rented a place on the south side of the beach near my favorite spot and the St. Andrews picnic area. I wanted, no, I needed to be close to my dolphins.

Coming through the sliding glass doors at the back of the house, I took off my flip flops, dusted the sand from my feet, leaned my beach chair against the outside wall, and put away my backpack and towel. I meandered into the shower and processed how weird that the money my dad had put in a special bank account years ago for me would be used for this. Maybe my dad knew that it would be needed for an emergency someday and this definitely felt like one. Actually, it was probably worse than that. It felt like I was a big pile of dust on the floor in a powdery heap of crumbled brokenness. *How could he have known?* I dried off and put on a fresh pink tank top with matching shorts. Climbing into bed from pure mental and physical exhaustion, deep sleep came fast.

ERIN

The sun shone so brightly into the room that it was impossible to see the time on the old-fashioned clock next to the bed. On previous visits I'd race the sun to see who would show up first on the beach, but I didn't have the energy to play this morning. My eyes felt so heavy, as if someone were forcing them shut. As I awakened, the responsible part of my brain kicked in and I turned on my cell phone to find eight missed calls. Figures. I did leave town pretty quickly. Luckily, my boss had been understanding when I asked for time off at the last minute. Over the last eleven years I had built a solid relationship with my boss, Don, who was the founder of the company. The best part, at the time, was it was near Thom.

During those years, I worked my way up to Vice President of Public Relations for Franklin Advertising. The days were long and travel sometimes intense, but Thom had never seemed to mind too much. If anything, I think he liked my drive. All my life I was the constant overachiever looking to get ahead, or now that I look back on it, maybe it was for the attention. The apple didn't fall far from the tree. My mom was one of those women who always did things opposite of what the book called for. When most women were stay-at-home moms, she earned her real estate license. Not as a part-time job or to "dabble" in it. Nothing was ever part time with my mom. Well, except for raising me. Not that she meant to be that way, but you know how some women are just "made" to be the full-time mom? That wasn't mine. Sure, I think she wanted me. I just think she also wanted other things more. She didn't just want to be a real estate agent. Instead, she had to be 'The one and only of choice.'

Most times the only way I could get my mom to take notice was to get an award at school, be the star actor in the school play, or sing the national anthem at the homecoming football game; probably because it gave her the opportunity to have the notoriety, too. "Look," she would say, "My daughter Erin just got the lead in the musical!" It was like I was her opening topic of conversation with someone she wanted to talk to or meet. Maybe that's not really the way it was, but that's how it felt, looking through a teenager's eyes.

Dad was happy running his accounting practice that Grandpa had established. He didn't crave the spotlight like mom did. He was comfortable with just being, well, comfortable. No surprises. No drama. In fact, the more routine things were the more he seemed to like it. Sometimes my friends would say "Gosh, your dad is so cool. He never misses anything that you do." It was true. He would always put me first above any work, or at least from what I can remember. It was like he had the "mom gene" of the nurturer infused into him. I don't know what drove me crazier at times while growing up, my mom's workaholic personality with her constant drive for perfection or my dad's practicality of life.

No wonder I had days of total confusion. My mom made me feel as if my self-esteem was connected to being number one, while my dad's influence centered on love and family as the only things that mattered. Maybe that was their secret to their thirty-nine years together. They were so different that maybe when they looked at each other they admired the qualities the other person had because they didn't possess them. They definitely blended.

It was different with Thom. We met during my junior year of college while he was a legal assistant at a local law firm, studying for his bar exam. A few years older than me, his passion for business sent me over the edge. I remember meeting him at a local Irish pub in downtown Charlotte one weekend. My friend Sam introduced us. It was like Thom wanted to set the world on fire and whoever was ready to join him would carry the torch right alongside him. We seemed to share the same ambitious nature that propelled us into the fast lane. During my senior year of college, we commuted between Charlotte and Duke, spending time together when his work schedule allowed. I knew that his career came first, but it was something I was comfortable with since I had that type of relationship with my mom. After graduation, I was fortunate to get a job offer from Franklin Advertising, where I had done my internship.

Don Franklin had taken me under his wing. It probably didn't come that big of a surprise when I asked Don for a leave of absence at the last minute. I knew it was a lot to ask, but my executive assistant, Kim, could hold down the fort. She was so well groomed that she really needed to move out of her position and onto my consultant team. Even with my dad's cancer and the miscarriage, I didn't take much time off. Work was my solution to avoid feelings that I didn't want to deal with. But for whatever reason, I hit the wall with what just happened in my marriage. It was like all these little stacks of wood, like a Jenga game, were being piled on. By adding one more to the stack, the entire tower came crashing down. I was suffocating. The city of Charlotte, North Carolina instantly became too small for me, and I had to escape from it.

Don asked if I would be available after a couple of weeks to work remotely, but I couldn't even think clearly enough to answer him. I looked at the missed calls on my cell. Two from Thom, three from Laura, and another three from my mom prompted me to turn it off altogether so I wouldn't even see the activity. I had to. Why did I come here? I came here to take back my life. I came here to get clear and find my way back to me. Listening to voicemails could wait, and if I really had to be honest with myself, I just couldn't deal with any more conflict right now.

QUIET. Couldn't things just be quiet so I could figure out what my own voice was saying? How did my voice get drowned out by all the other voices all these years? Just thinking about it made me more determined to find them; those beautiful creatures that I could talk to and who seemed to listen to me on a level that only God would understand.

God. Well, that was another story. I lost my faith in God somewhere along the way, too. I wonder if that happened before or after I started losing my inner voice. Pushing those nagging thoughts aside, I put on my tennis skirt, t-shirt, sun visor, and running shoes. Opening the sliding glass door I hit the beach, leaving my cell phone on the nightstand.

CHAPTER 3

ERIN

A blast of cool air hit me in the face as I walked in the door to the house. Even though it was March, I had worked up a sweat. The run on the beach gave me a fresh perspective. I was never the type to feel sorry for myself, so why start now? The dolphin pods I'd seen reminded me of that as I watched them swim in circles. Suddenly they'd change direction. If they were looking to feed, they would change their path and location. I could do that. No problem. Amazing how sure of myself I could feel after a run.

I looked around the beach house and mentally took it in. The place wasn't that small but definitely more cramped than our house back in Charlotte. *"Did I just say our house?"* I thought to myself with a feeling of nostalgia. This place felt cozy, like the home was actually hugging me. Like it was protecting me from what might be coming. Built in the 1970's, it was a ranch house with some outdated features. The windows and front door looked original. What I loved about the place was the huge great room, a living and dining area combination, framed by a wall of floor-to-ceiling windows. The living area had a blue and white striped sofa, two blue linen comfy chairs and a coffee table. In the left corner of the room sat a writing desk with a white wicker beach-style chair.

An upright piano caught my eye instantly. I hadn't played in forever. I started taking lessons at the age of five, as my mom said it would be a good thing for me. She claims that I could carry a tune since I was old enough to talk. She even said I hummed to music before I was able to make out words. Piano lessons became a necessary chore, but I really loved writing music. *"Weird. When did I stop writing?"* I walked over to it and sat down on the bench, raising the lid. My hands instinctively reached for the keys. It felt like meeting an old friend you were unsure of embracing. *"Erin, you need to play."* It was this whisper in my ear or inside my heart. It had been so long. I might have known the key, but I didn't know the music within me anymore. I thickly swallowed as I sat quietly. My heart ached from wanting to express itself, but not knowing how.

I shook off my feelings as best as I could and walked into the kitchen to get some water. The homeowner must love to cook because the kitchen was a culinary dream. Definitely not the old-style seventies layout. They had knocked down a wall, opening the entire room up to the great room, separated only by a long breakfast bar. The breakfast bar and countertop were fresh white and blue speckled granite that curved around to a deep, double sink. As my eyes continued to travel through space, I noticed the high-end, stainless-steel appliances and the convection oven above the main oven. With most of the other rooms ignored in updating, this room had definitely been well thought out.

Jack at Ocean Realty told me that I could lease the place through the end of April, but if I wanted to renew it till the start of summer, I would need to let him know. He said if someone inquired about renting it for May, he would let me know. I was able to get the place pretty easily because the owners rented the house only by the month. Jack told me that the owners would be there from the fourth of July through the second week of September. They had stayed here every summer over the last twenty-six years.

Slicing a lemon and dropping it into my glass of ice water, I took stock of the kitchen thinking I better do an official grocery run. This kitchen brought out my creative side. I wanted to cook something special. As if inventing a dish or creating something mouth-watering would in turn reinvent me. I had never been much of a cook, but Thom wasn't home most evenings anyway. When he was working on a case, meeting clients for dinner, or just catching up on paperwork, I found walking to one of the local dining places was easier. In the little area of Dilworth, I could find what I wanted pretty easily on my own. But being here for an extended period of time might force me to change my ways. On the island there were only a few places to eat for dinner and only one pizza delivery place. There was a new convention center that had brought in new hotels and a couple of new places to eat, but the variety wasn't like Charlotte.

"Maybe this is your opportunity to try your hand at cooking", said the little voice. Ignoring the inner pull that music (and not necessarily cooking) was something I should reconnect with. I had always been creative when I was little but over time, I had unknowingly gotten away from it; like bundling it up, packing it away in a box, and sliding it on the top shelf in a dark closet. Not sure why or how, but maybe life, little by little, has done that to me. Thinking of writing music would mean exposing pain, and that just wasn't an option right now. Cooking was much safer.

"Ok girl, you are going to make something fun and special for yourself this week." I said literally out loud, so the house could hear me too.

The house phone jolted me from my daydreaming and self-talk. *Did I give anyone this number? I don't think so.* "Hello?" I said cautiously, not sure who it could be, but at least knowing it wasn't someone that I didn't want to talk to, just yet.

"Well at least you picked up the phone, because obviously you aren't returning calls from your cell phone messages." She was getting right to the point. "I had to find out from work where you had gone. Everyone was so tight lipped you would have thought that you worked for the CIA. What is going on, darling?" Her properly southern accent blended with the European sophistication passed down through her family always gave off an air that she was better than others. "I called Thom, and he said you had gone away for a few days, but by the way he said it, I had a feeling that he wasn't telling me the whole story. So, tell me, what's going on?"

I stood there a moment, my body leaning against the cold granite countertop to stabilize myself. "Mom, I am so glad you called. I just got in yesterday and haven't had time to let you know. I have been so busy I haven't even had my cell phone on. I didn't even see your missed call."

I lied. The lying became easy because I was also lying to myself. It kept my emotions at bay. "Really mom, there isn't anything to worry about. I just wanted to take some vacation time and relax for a bit."

There was no reason to go into the whole situation with Thom and Laura right now. I didn't need her judgmental viewpoint on things, and I didn't want to have to retell the entire story. How I came home from lunch to retrieve a client folder only to walk through my door to the sound of laughter and other sounds coming from our bedroom. Quickly I changed the focus of the conversation back over to her.!

"So, mom, how's work going? Are you working on any big sales right now?"

"Well, you know darling, one moment the market is improving and the next moment they are saying we are still in a slump, so no one seems to know what the market is really going to do over the next couple of years. But I do have a new listing and that's good. It's a doctor's home here in Old Salem. He is moving to work at the Cleveland clinic. It's a wonderful home. I am hoping it will sell fast, but historical homes can move slower than the lower-end price points." I listened to her rambling on about the market and reflected that I was glad she had this passion since my dad died just two years ago. At the same time, it was aggravating that she seemed so polished and resilient even after Dad's passing. Shoot, it seemed like that was built into her DNA. All of the blabbing gave me an itch that I couldn't scratch.

"Hey mom, can we catch up a bit later? I am going to meet some friends for dinner and watch the sunset. I'll call in the next couple of days, okay? Oh, and don't worry about me. I am just taking some time for myself." I tried to sound lighthearted. That was the goal anyway, but not sure if I pulled it off. I guess my mom might have picked up on the strain in my voice or maybe she did believe me, and she let it go. "Ok darling, but please call and let me know how you are doing. I am worried about you," she said with thick concern in her tone.

Funny, at this point I was worried about myself, too.

CHAPTER 4

SOPHIA

As I hung up the phone, I knew Erin wasn't telling me everything. A mother knows these things about their children. It's like as soon as we give birth a sixth sense is turned on. I knew better than to push her though. Ever since she was born, she has had a mind of her own. She was such an organizing fanatic like her father, having to have everything in the same place no matter what. But she also had this creative side where her heart took over her brain. She probably didn't know it, but she got her creative side from me. The way she would write songs in her room with her door closed; or write poems in a journal she would carry around, until it would practically fall apart in her hands. What was interesting, though, is that she never shared them with anyone, let alone me. It was like a part of her soul she wanted to keep hidden.

I love Erin more than my own breath but, I don't think she felt that. I could tell by the way she looked at me, she thought I only cared about my work. During her teenage years she had mentioned it in the midst of a few arguments. To this day it still stung. But she didn't know the real reason I took up real estate. Truth is, I never thought I would work full time after I had children. I remember meeting Matthew at a social mixer while attending the all-girl college, Sweetbriar. I was studying to be a schoolteacher. Matthew was at UVA studying to be an accountant. Since he was from Winston-Salem, we settled there so he could join his father's accounting practice. It had grown pretty sizable under his dad's direction, and he was coming in as a full partner with the firm. We were married for eight years before Erin was born, settling into the routine of life. Matthew was building his client base, and I was teaching second grade. We wanted children right away, but I had a hard time getting pregnant. So, by the time we found out that we were having a baby, we were ecstatic. It was like everything was coming together and when she was born our lives took on a new meaning. It was no longer about the two of us but about building a family. We tried to have more children, but it just didn't happen for us.

It changed the week of Christmas break when Erin was just seven years old. Matthew had been feeling under the weather the previous couple of months and thought the long hours were catching up to him. He dismissed his upset stomach and multiple trips to the bathroom in the middle of the night as stress, but after losing twenty-five pounds in six weeks, I forced him to see his doctor. I thought he might have a food allergy, but even though he was just in his early forties, they recommended he have some extensive tests run. Luckily, they said that the cancer in his colon was caught quickly. The surgery eliminated the need for chemotherapy, but he still had to go through radiation treatments. We caught it in time.

His experience shook me to the core. It made me realize that if something happened to Matthew where would that leave Erin and me financially? Sure, I could teach school, but teacher salaries didn't pay much. I wanted her to have the best in life and live in the house she was born and raised in. If anything happened, his parents would help us out. But I didn't want to live a life so dependent on someone else. A friend suggested I get my real estate license. I really liked the idea of a flexible schedule to care for Erin. It was a perfect fit. Little did I know how much I was going to love it. Real estate opened a whole new world for me. Seeing the different houses and how they were decorated fascinated me. I felt like I was contributing on a bigger level and really helping people. It let me show my creative side in designing brochures and staging houses. As time went on, I realized I could be near Erin while promoting my business. I started to work her school bake sales, sponsor the sports team and volunteer to help out at other events, like school plays. Basically, anything that would help my business while keeping an eye on her.

I didn't realize how my work had affected my relationship with Erin. Through her elementary school years, I worked, and she seemed to be doing great. But in the summer of her eighth-grade year things changed. Before I knew it, she didn't want to get in the car with me. Growing up she loved playing "Realtor." She would walk through the house and pretend she was my partner. It was quite adorable. But when that teenage world hit, she didn't seem to want to be around me at all. I remember one day after school I offered to take her to the mall and go shopping and she said, "Mom, it's not cool to go shopping with your mom. Just give me some money and drop me and my friends off." As time continued, she seemed to pull herself away and be more distant. I knew most thirteen-year-old girls began fighting for their independence, but I didn't realize how much it could hurt. She would come home from school, walk upstairs, shut her door and barely come out for dinner. Sometimes it was a fight just to get her down for a family meal. Matthew didn't seem to worry about it. He would just say, "Let her be. She is just growing up, sweetheart. You have to give her space."

That was easy for him to say. Matthew and Erin had a different kind of relationship. There would be Saturdays where he would take her to her soccer event while I worked. They would stay out all day, going out for breakfast before her game and then either shopping or watching college football in the afternoons. Their bond was something unique and many times I felt like the third wheel. I wasn't jealous because it made me happy to see them so close. At the same time, I craved the connection he had with her. It was something I couldn't seem to make happen in the way he did. That was Matthew for you, though. It was like the cancer scare changed him. It changed the way he looked at his mortality and his life. His passion for living was rooted inside him at the deepest level. Even though he worked his job, he took time off to be with Erin as much as possible. Owning the accounting firm gave him a flexible schedule and he would be the one who would volunteer to carpool to events, such as the regional championship games. You could tell by the way he looked at her, he didn't trust how long he had. He made every minute count.

Maybe that is why I threw myself into work because I couldn't compete with that. Honestly after her sophomore year of high school, I had resigned myself to the realization that they had a closeness she and I would never share. I loved her but reaching out to her only to get rejected was more than I could bear. There was a huge wall between us and as the years went on it grew taller and thicker. There were days that I counted down the calendar wishing college would come quickly so I wouldn't have to deal with the feeling of walking on eggshells in my own home. Deep down, I wanted her to like me, and it seemed as though she didn't. If only I could go back in time and make it different, I would. I wish I had known how to handle things better, but that wall had grown so thick with layer upon layer of disconnection, it became easier for us to pretend that it wasn't there.

On the phone with her I had a feeling that something serious was going on. Her assistant at the office said she was taking a four-week vacation and Erin never did that. She would take three or four long weekend trips a year but never a full week, much less a whole month. Probably because that husband of hers was such a workaholic. I wish

Matthew was here. Tears stung my eyes. He would know what to do or what to say.

I felt lost. Lost with connecting to Erin and lost that I was all alone now. I thought my work was enough. But now at sixty-four years old, I realized that it wasn't anymore. If only I would have recognized this earlier.

I put my phone back in my purse and looked into the mirror to make sure my hair and makeup were presentable. Only I could see the loneliness and pain behind my eyes. I hoped that no one else could.

CHAPTER 5

ERIN

The conversation with my mom went like I knew it would, forced and limited. It had been like that for so long, I expected it. It was like we had turned into strangers without even realizing that it happened. I remember the first day of college at Duke when they had dropped me off. Mom was so distant she barely wanted to hug me goodbye. Dad was the middleman smoothing out the rough edges between us. It's sad. I don't even remember how it developed between Mom and me, but it was there. I never felt she understood me. Didn't she realize that I was always doing things to impress her? Childless at thirty-four and not presenting her with the grandchild she wanted felt like another failure.

I remember the day of my wedding when mom was helping me get dressed, she kept asking, "Do I look okay in this outfit? Are the flowers set correctly? What about the lighting?" I remember thinking, *Seriously? Can we just have one day that is not focused on you? I mean I am the one getting married here.* It was something I got used to as time went on.

Mom was always concerned with outward appearances. She always made sure she was pulled together, down to her manicured nails and lipstick. It worked, too. She was remarkably striking. Even in her early sixties she looked like someone in her late forties. Her short blond hair with long layers softly shaping her face complimented her steel–blue eyes and shapely figure. She had told me more than once that she won the Miss Apple festival in her hometown of Lincolnton, North Carolina and she was very proud of that.

I got myself ready to go to the Shrimp Boil, an outdoor restaurant on the water that serves Georgia wild shrimp which is to die for. Looking in the mirror I assessed myself. I am not sure if I got her looks or not. Folks would say how much I favored my mom, but I couldn't compete with her perfectionism. I had her eyes but also the auburn brown hair and tall physique of my dad. She was tight and petite. I blow-dried my hair thinking it was in dire need of a trim. I would have to put that on my 'to do' list. I had a feeling there might be a lot on my 'to do' list. I didn't want to think about that right now. I was going to meet Shelia and catch up. It had been a long while since we'd seen each other but she was one of those friends that even though you didn't see each other physically, you picked right up where you left off.

I remember the first day I met her. It had been my first trip to Jekyll to meet with Patti in sales and other members of the executive team of the Jekyll Island Club Hotel. I was going to pitch them an advertising campaign focused on bringing in special events and offering unique venues. It was about five-thirty in the morning and I had hit the beach for an early morning run. I was wearing my earbuds and listening to my playlist, only to almost run headfirst into a vehicle that was a cross between a golf cart and a four-wheeler. I couldn't imagine who would be out on the beach in the dark before the sunrise, much less in that contraption; but sure enough the headlights in my eyes caught my attention before I ran into her. Thank God she was paying attention, swerving out of my way only to yell, "Hey watch out!"

"Oh my gosh, I am so sorry," I said as I took out my earplugs. "I must have been zoning out to my music and not paying attention. I didn't think anyone would be out here at this time."

"No problem,» she smiled at me with warm eyes. «You scared me too. I thought you heard my engine. But then I realized you weren't going to stop running towards me. I am on turtle patrol this week," she said.

"Turtle patrol?" I asked. "Oh, that's right, I read about that when I was doing my research to come down here. You guys have all these rules on the island about it, right?" I asked inquisitively.

"Yes, and you're breaking one of them right now, by using that flashlight. You are supposed to only use a flashlight that emits a red light. Using normal flashlights on the beach can confuse the turtles. They follow the light of the moon to get back to the water after laying their eggs. The same applies when the babies hatch. They have to follow the moon's light to get into the water." I could see the passion in her eyes as she kept talking. "Right now, we have seventeen nests on the island but it's only May, so I suspect that this year we will have well over a hundred."

"Wow," I said. «Do you do this full time?»

"No", she said. "I am what folks call a research volunteer. This is how we keep tabs on the turtles and make sure there are no left-over moats from the sandcastles and such. We patrol during the overnight hours and keep watch to see if they create any new nests. When we find one that needs to be marked, we stake it and cover it with special netting to protect it from predators such as crabs and birds. I got hooked on it when I moved here from Darien." You could see her radiant smile explode as she explained her mission.

"I'm so sorry about the flashlight I had no idea. So, what kind of work do you do here?" I asked.

"Here, you can put this red plastic over it. That should take care of it," she said handing it to me with a little rubber band to wrap around my flashlight. "I own a shop in the historic area called Reflections. Basically, we have tons of different types of art and novelties that tourists like. I love it, but what I am doing right now is my passion. I love our turtles. They are like my family. It's so remarkable that a turtle comes back to build her nest in the same spot where she hatched. I am mesmerized by the whole experience."

We were friends from that day forward. There would be periods of time we didn't talk much by phone and just messaged each other on social media or via text. But I felt this soul sister connection with her every time we were together. I looked down at my watch and didn't realize how long I had been daydreaming about our first meeting. I pulled my hair back into a ponytail and quickly put on a fresh coat of mascara, a dab of lip gloss and rushed out the door to meet her. I had a lot to tell her and didn't know where to start. Hopefully it would be easier after a few shrimp and a beer to wash them down.

CHAPTER 6

ERIN

Being on island time had its advantages. I arrived a couple of minutes late but knew Shelia would be fine with it. It helped that her demeanor was like the tide, always able to go with the flow. I admire that about her and was a bit jealous of how she could let things be and not fight against the current. She was the Ying of my Yang and every time I came down for work stuff, we would start out by meeting at the Shrimp Boil to catch up on our lives.

As I walked to the end of the boardwalk, I saw her seated outside. Her straight blond hair was pulled back into a ponytail, and she wore round, bejeweled sunglasses. Even though it was early spring her long legs looked tanned against her crisp white shorts and her white and light blue striped collared shirt. More than ever, it felt good to see her. I had felt totally alone, but when I saw her at a table under the wooden gazebo, she gave me a sense of kinship.

Shelia gave me a huge smile with her arms open for a big hug. "Hey girl! It's so good to see you! How's it going?"

Once she looked in my eyes she knew. She cocked her head and looked at me with concerned eyes, "Something is wrong. What is it?"

I could feel the tears behind my eyes dying to spring forward, but I kept them at bay. "How about we get some shrimp ordered and relax a bit. We have plenty of time to talk and I can fill you in, but first I want to hear about you and how things are going." I had gotten so very good at changing the subject.

"Well, let's see," she said. "I am gearing up for the summer volunteer season and am excited about that. Over the winter I decided to volunteer more hours, specifically at the turtle center. There are about twelve turtles that we are currently nursing back to health. Three of them were injured by boats last fall. And, I have been involved in this program at my church that I have fallen in love with. I'll have to fill you in on that, but first, I want to know what's up with you."

"How about your shop?" Deflecting again.

"The store is doing awesome! We are getting more interest in the local art we feature in the renovated loft. There is a local artist that has helped me get more established in the market, so that has brought in business. Over the last couple of years, he has become popular around here. I don't know if you know him or not. Scott Fuller?"

Last summer when I was consulting at the Jekyll Island Club hotel, I heard he was making a name for himself here. The hotel put on an art and wine event showcasing Fuller and other local artists. Our agency handled the marketing campaign for it. I only viewed his work by email attachments when we were drawing up the magazine ads and website content featuring his work. He was known for painting landscapes and wildlife of the low country, as well as the private islands off the Southern coast.

"I know of him," I said. "From what I remember he seemed to have an eye for capturing nature."

"He just bought a house over on Bliss Lane," she continued. "He was getting so popular that he decided to sell his house in St. Simons and move over here where it's quieter. He keeps his boat at the landing and when I talk to him, he is either coming in or going out on it. He seems to be adventurous. He's a quiet guy, but we have become good friends. He's come out with me a couple of times on turtle patrol to observe since pictures aren't allowed without permission."

"Any romance sparks?" I couldn't help but ask.

"Scott?" Shelia laughed. "No way. Although I don't know what woman in her right mind wouldn't want to get his attention, but we don't have that vibe, you know. It's kind of like a brother thing… Not sure why, but it is. I just wish he had a friend for me. That would be right on. Enough about me. What are you doing here in March? You always come the third weekend of May. Are you here for work?"

I wish…

"Not exactly. I don't know where to start." The tears welled up. "It's Thom. Well, not just Thom. It's… well…" The tears started spilling over my lashes and down my cheeks.

"Have things not improved between the two of you? I know that he has been really working a lot since your miscarriage. Is that still happening?" she asked, taking my hand and adding, "You have been on my mind, and I have been praying for you."

I did not want to get into a conversation about prayer because I didn't believe in it like when I was a kid. I just answered her question. "I found him in bed with Laura."

"Your friend, Laura?" she asked wide-eyed.

"Yeah" … I didn't know how to continue on.

"Oh my, Erin. I am so sorry. What are you going to do? How can I help?"

"I don't know. I feel numb right now. Thom and I have been having trouble, but I thought it was just because of the baby and all the things that have happened over the last couple of years. I thought we'd get through it. But I am just really angry. How could Laura do this to me? Who would betray their friend by sleeping with their husband?" I wasn't posing it as a question as much as making a statement.

"I didn't think he and Laura were that close. You told me you thought they never really got along."

"Yeah, it was like that in the beginning. I remember how she was aggravated when he and I started getting serious in college. She felt that I didn't have time for her anymore. But they started getting along over the last couple of years."

The last couple of years, I thought to myself. *How long has this been going on?* I didn't even consider it an affair, but now the thought crept into the shadows of my mind. It made me nauseous to think about it.

"You and Laura have been friends practically forever, right?" Shelia asked.

"Well, pretty much. We met during our freshman year at Duke and shared an apartment our sophomore year. She and I were roommates all the way through college, and she was my maid of honor at our wedding. Did you know she was with me the night I met him? Even then you could tell they didn't get along. I always thought it was because they were both studying law and were competitive. You know she is an attorney too, right?"

"Oh yes," she replied. "Maybe they are meant for each other. They say you can't trust lawyers so maybe this proves it. Have you talked to either one of them since this happened?"

"No," I said. "It literally just happened. It's been a whirlwind. I needed some breathing room to get my emotions in check. I don't want to appear to either one of them like I am losing it. I don't want to give them that."

"So, what is your next step?" she asked, cocking her head sideways communicating her genuine concern.

"I got lucky enough to rent a house here for a bit. I took vacation time that I had banked, and my boss really understands what's going on. I was able to tell him in confidence. That is the benefit of working for him for so long. I told him I would be willing to work from here if the firm gets in a jam. One of our big accounts is still the Club Hotel, so I think he may have me check in on them. Plus, we are bidding on a new project with a hotel in St. Simons. Quite honestly, I am just grateful that he is working around my drama. Most bosses wouldn't do that."

"That's for sure. But it sounds like you may be more than just another employee. I mean, didn't he mention last year about bringing you in as a partner or owner or something?" she asked, working through her second iced tea while I nursed the beer in my hands, with little desire to drink or eat.

"Yeah. He mentioned it. He wants to retire in another ten years, and I think he wants me to run things while he holds a seat on the board as an advisor." I stopped right then because work was the farthest thing from my mind. It was another indicator that nothing in my life seemed secure anymore. I mean, here I was side slapped with this affair so maybe my discernment in all areas of my life was broken. Work was my identity. It was the one thing I had… my professional identity.

"I tell you what," Shelia said. "It sounds like you have some free time on your hands, Girly-Girl, so why don't you come and help me at the shop tomorrow? I have to clean out some inventory to make room for some of the new art from the Art Festival a couple of weeks ago. Scott mentioned some brand-new paintings that he hasn't shown anyone yet and I get first dibs to showcase them. It would sure be a big help to me. And it will keep your mind off things. Come on. Want to?"

"Why not. Sounds like it may be what the doctor is calling for. What time do you want me there?" Even though I loved hanging out with her I didn't really feel like being social, but I knew sitting in the house sulking wasn't going to do me any good either.

"How about ten-thirty? We can work for a bit, take a lunch break and then finish up. It will be fun! It will give you something else to think about. And, girlfriend, with your eye for marketing and advertising, maybe you can give me some free advice!" She chuckled, making me genuinely smile back at her. She was some good medicine for my soul. Just being around her gave me warmth.

"Sounds good." We wrapped up our dinner, exchanged quick hugs and got in our separate cars. I was excited about seeing her the next morning.

As she pulled away, she put down her window and said, "Erin, I don't want you to think I am pushing anything on you, but I do want you to know that even if you feel like you are in this alone, I am here for you. God is always there for you too, okay?"

I trusted that she was, but I wasn't sure if I believed that God was, because why would He be there for me when I hadn't even acknowledged him in forever? Looking into her eyes showed meaning behind her words. Shelia gave me something that I couldn't give myself right now — and that was hope.

CHAPTER 7

ERIN

I swung the door open to the shop and heard the jingling bells attached to the door. I thought of the movie 'It's a Wonderful Life' and when the little girl said, "Teacher says every time a bell rings an angel gets his wings." *I wonder if that's true.* I thought of my dad and every Christmas taking time to watch that movie of 'It's a Wonderful Life.'

Shelia came bounding out through the back of the store with her hair in a barrette so it was away from her eyes. "Great, you made it! Hope you are ready to get your hands dirty. I really need to get some things done and I have been waiting for someone to give me an extra set of hands."

"At your service!" I gave her an honorary salute, actually feeling a bit giddy being around her. "What do you need me to do?" I looked down at my tan cargo shorts and felt very grateful I didn't wear my white ones that I had been contemplating. However now I wish I would have pulled my hair back into a ponytail since it looked like I might work up a sweat. After looking at Shelia's straight hair it gave me a desire to wash my hair, dry it slowly and flat iron it. I had been cursed, or some would argue blessed, with wavy hair. At the beach it usually wouldn't cooperate, but since it was spring and humidity wasn't in full swing, I thought maybe I could attempt it.

"Help me get these empty boxes from the back up toward the front of the door. I am changing out some of our items to get ready for the summer market."

Following her to the back of the store I stopped suddenly, awestruck at a wall of paintings in front of me. I'm not sure how many minutes I was standing there when she said, "They are breathtaking aren't they?"

"They sure are," I said. "I don't think I had ever seen paintings that felt like I could step inside of it."

Out of all the paintings there was one that drew me in close. It was a large painting with a view of someone sitting on a boat overlooking an uninhabited island. On the island were three horses with their necks bowed downward. They were grazing on sea oats while their hoofs were invisible in the sand. To the left of the island was a larger view of the sky featuring an orange and pink melding of colors with white wispy clouds. In between the boat and the shore of the island was a dolphin jumping out of the water while three other dolphin fins were peeking out of the water beneath. The painting sparkled and looked so alive that I felt I was sitting on the boat watching it in real time.

Just about that time the bell rang again at the front door of the shop and I turned around to say hello to the customer. But when I saw him, I knew who he was by the picture in the magazine layout we had done.

"Hi. Is Shelia around?" He asked me casually.

"Umm, yes." I stammered a bit. "She is in the back. I can get her for you if you like. Can I say who is asking for her?" I continued, even though I knew who he was. He looked to be about six foot two inches. His dark brown hair had sun kissed flecks of gold that gave it a shimmer. His five o'clock shadow, most likely left over from yesterday, made his amber eyes stand out even more.

"That would be great. Can you let her know Scott is here and that I have some things in the back of my truck she might want to see."

I went to the back storage room. "Shelia, that Scott Fuller guy is here for you. He says that he has some things for you in the back of his truck that you might want to see."

"Oh really?" She said surprised. "I wasn't expecting him until the end of the week."

She took the initiative of heading out first while I followed behind her. "Scott! It's great to see you! I thought you weren't going to stop by until the end of the week. I hear you have something to show me. Now you have me curious!" Her enthusiasm was infectious.

"Well, I am going up to Savannah for a few days to visit my agent and the owner of another gallery. I didn't want to delay seeing you so I thought I would come here first."

"You're the best!", said Shelia. "Now you have piqued my interest. I have got to see them. You know I had someone stop in just yesterday looking at your Sapelo Island painting. They seemed really hot about it. They are supposed to stop this afternoon again. By the way," she continued, "this is my good friend, Erin. Erin, this is Scott Fuller."

"I thought you might be," I said. "I recognize your picture from an advertisement my firm did for the Wine and Art event at the Club Hotel last year. It is very nice to meet you." He looked into my eyes and held his gaze. It really made me uncomfortable to the point where it forced me to look away. It was like he was peering into my private thoughts and right now, above anytime, I didn't feel comfortable with that.

"Nice to meet you too, Erin," he said. "Where are you visiting from?"

"I live in Charlotte, but I am renting a house on the south side near St. Andrews beach. I have known Shelia for a while. We actually met five years ago when I was down here for work. I have been coming back every year since." I knew I was rambling on but found that I couldn't stop myself. "You do amazing work."

"Thank you," he said, sounding like he didn't really believe it. "I can't take all the credit." With that he was quiet for what seemed like forever while appearing to be somewhere else for a moment. "So, Shelia, ready to take a peek?"

"Sure! Let's have at it!" She said. "Come on, don't you want to see too?" With that push, I fell in line behind them.

He walked to the back of his truck and took each piece out carefully while laying them up against the body of the vehicle. Each told its own story without words. One painting was set in the night, lit by a full moon, which in turn lit up the water and the sky above. Out of a breaking wave there was the head and a quarter of a turtle's body emerging out of the water, allowing the waves to push her on to the shore.

The second was before daybreak with a focus on a turtle's nest in the middle of a hatch, with the little turtles all stacked up upon each other, each using the other as a ladder to emerge from the nest.

The other two were of sunsets over the marshland, but it was the fifth one that caused me to catch my breath. The painting was of the ocean but showcasing what lay underneath the surface. Light from above was penetrating the surface and casting rays of light into the depth of the water. The focal point was on one dolphin. She had big eyes that popped off the canvas. When I stared at her I felt a connection that I couldn't explain even if I wanted to. She looked at me as if she knew the feelings in my heart and the questions I had in my mind. It was like someone had entered my soul and had painted the image of how my dolphin soul mate would be.

"How much for this painting?" I surprised myself.

Shelia and Scott exchanged looks and then back at me. "Erin, I didn't know you collected art." Would you really want to buy one right now with so much going on?" said Shelia. I guess she must have realized what had come out of her mouth by the look I shot her. I had no desire for any indication about my personal life. "Scott", She asked, "what are these going to go for?"

Well, my agent usually prices it. I have to get the exact quote for each one. I'll have those for you by end of day. I try not to get into that part of the business," he said with an uncomfortable tone.

"I think it is amazing that your art is in such high demand now!" exclaimed Shelia. "Erin, did you know that one of his paintings just sold here for nine thousand."

I really felt a connection with this dolphin painting. I couldn't explain why, then logic seeped into my brain. *Erin, you can't spend money on a painting like that! There is too much up in the air for you to make that kind of purchase. If it's meant to be it will be available when the time is right. But for now, you just can't do it. You must be practical.*

I knew my logic was right. I had just spent money on my rental house and who knew what the coming weeks or months would hold for me. It was not the time to be investing in art, much less buying something out of pure emotion.

"Wow, I had no idea. Not that I mean any disrespect because they are truly beautiful. But I guess I won't be buying that anytime soon," I said with a faint laugh behind it.

"Yeah, that is how I felt too when I first started painting," He replied. "What put me on the map was that gallery event at the hotel. Folks came from all over, as far north as Indiana and as far south as the Florida Keys. Before I knew it people were purchasing my art and then reselling it instantly for a profit. It's been busy for me ever since. Folks say I should make reprints of my paintings, but I haven't felt comfortable doing that just yet, although my agent is pushing for it pretty hard right now. She says it will give me leverage. I feel like each one is supposed to be its very own story and not to be duplicated. I don't know if I can really explain how I feel. But from what I hear, doing reprints is the nature of the business progression."

As he shared those words with Shelia and me, I could see in his eyes that he wasn't painting for the money. I felt that he was painting for a different purpose. Almost like he was trying to heal a deep wound within himself, and that painting was the medicine. Right then and there I thought *I need to find something like that to heal my wounds. I wonder how to discover that?* The voice inside me answered, *you have discovered it, Erin; years ago when you wrote your music. Remember?* I shook my head to brush off my feelings.

I couldn't explain it, but even though I had just met him today, I felt like I understood him. It was a connection that disturbed me to the very core of my being. I had to get out of the shop and the sooner the better. I didn't need another set of emotions to deal with.

"I tell you what Scott," Shelia said. "I will keep the dolphin picture and the two turtle pictures. I can't thank you enough for letting me have first pick as I am sure the Savannah gallery has a lot more foot traffic."

"My pleasure," said Scott. "After all, you were the first one to take my paintings and that goes a long way with me," he said with a sincere smile. "Will I see you at church on Sunday? You should bring Erin."

"Yeah Erin," Shelia said. "We have a good group to hang out with. It would be fun for you to meet some other folks in our age group and get you out of the house".

I didn't want to hurt her feelings or give a bad impression to Scott, so I just kept my comment simple and easy. "I'll think about it. I still have some settling in to do." With that comment he turned back to me and studied me a little too closely for comfort, but I tried to brush it off. "It was nice meeting you, Scott."

"You too, Erin. I hope to see you around." With that, he got back in his truck and drove off.

I was grateful for his departure, so I didn't go back on my word helping Shelia with her inventory. I worked with such focus and determined energy Shelia didn't know what to think of it, but she was grateful I had come.

"Wow," she said, "I can't believe we finished all the inventory today. It would have taken me four days by myself. I know who to call now!" She laughed. It made me feel good to help her and put my energy into helping someone else with their challenges. It got my mind off my own. "How about coming over and having some dinner at my place tonight?" she asked.

"I'd love to," I yawned, "but I think my body is worn out. Can I take a rain check? I hear a bubble bath calling my name."

"Sure thing." said Shelia. "Give me a call tomorrow if you want. Oh, and no pressure but think about church, okay?"

"Um. I'm just not into the religion thing. I don't think the church thing is really for me."

She smiled but didn't say anything, giving me a brief, firm hug.

I left hoping not to dream about my dolphin or the intriguing man that had painted it. It was my dolphin in that painting. It was already calling my name, wanting me to take it home.

CHAPTER 8

ERIN

It felt good to wake up rested. Over the last few days, I developed a routine of getting up thirty-five minutes before the sunrise. I'd pack up a backpack, beach chair, blanket, thermos of coffee, and a bottle of water. This morning was no exception. It felt good to not be tied to my phone and to anyone.

As I walked along the wooded path to the beach, I knew exactly where I was going… to the point. On a map it was called Jekyll Point, but I don't know if anyone thought of it much. Most tourists didn't sunbathe at Jekyll Point due to the St. Andrews picnic area and the Glory Beach boardwalk being so close by. There were benches, picnic tables, and restroom facilities that drew people to St. Andrews. Coming out to Jekyll Point was my little slice of heaven. It took a bit of a walk or a short jog to get to it, but it was worth it. I had a panoramic view of nothing but water and sand. *There aren't many beaches like this anymore.* I settled into my favorite spot and decided not to go for a run yet rather just sit and watch the surf roll.

The sky was too beautiful this morning and I wanted to watch it come to life. You could tell it was going to be a unique sunrise. There was a saying 'red clouds in morning, sailors' warning' so that must mean that rain was on its way. I settled into my beach chair, breathing in the crisp air and looking at the sun showing a pink sliver over the horizon.

"It's amazing how quickly the sun comes up once you start noticing, isn't it?" said a voice behind me. I turned around and there was Scott Fuller. I didn't know which was prettier, him or the sun as cliché as it sounded in my head. The light of the morning hit his face as he looked down on me.

"Good morning." I whispered, so as to not interfere with the serene atmosphere. "Want to sit and watch? It's happening and we don't want to miss it."

He sat down to my right. Together we sat in silence watching the dawn of this new day upon us. Although we didn't know each other well, I could feel an energy bouncing between us that I couldn't put my finger on. As the sun rose it was like it was a calling card for the wildlife to say good morning as well.

The flying fish started to jump in the water along the shore. It began the conversation between us.

"I wonder why fish jump like that. It's fascinating to watch."

"It is," he replied. "It's like they are dancing to their own music. I was reading about it in an Outer Banks magazine. They say that scientists aren't sure why they do it. It could be that they are getting pursued by a predator. But then again, why do dolphins jump? It might just be what they do."

"Last year when I was visiting, I saw a horseshoe crab up on shore. I thought he was stranded with the tide going out, so I threw him into the water. Then I ended up reading "that is what they do to mate with a partner," I said slightly embarrassed. "I sure messed up their chances."

"Well, I am sure they would forgive you… at some point, anyway," he joked.

As we laughed, I saw a pod of dolphins swimming north up toward the hotel area along the beach. "Look!" I pointed outward. He reached around in his backpack to grab something. Out came a camera with a long-range zoom lens and all the bells and whistles. "Wow, that is some camera," I said.

"Yeah," he shared, "I've had a love of photography since I was a kid. Now that I paint, a photo will sometimes help me reconnect to the emotion I felt at the time that I took it. I can bring that feeling into my work. It's more of a roadmap. The emotion is the piece of the puzzle that fills the story," he continued on, not afraid to share his thoughts with me. "I am not one of those that take thousands of photos in one day. Maybe I should, but I am just more selective. I can't explain it. I wait until the mood hits me or when I see something unique that maybe other people don't see. It's then that I start photographing. Like right now. May I take your picture? I know it's weird, but I love the contrast with the water and sky behind you," he asked with questioning yet determined eyes.

"I guess so," I said hesitantly.

"Great, take your hair out of your ponytail for me." As soon as I did, a rush of wind hit my face and blew my hair back. Like he anticipated it, he was already in position to take my picture. "Over there," he pointed, "the pod is to your left."

I shifted my body a bit more and pulled my knees up to my chest, with my head resting on my knees, like a child waiting for a gift at Christmas.

Like all good things that come in time, four dolphin fins came up out of the water in unison. He had been taking pictures, frame after frame.

I didn't care. It was one of those moments that I felt like the dolphins had come to let me know that they were watching over me; almost like a guardian angel would. I wondered deep down if they were trying to tell me something more.

Scott put the camera back in his bag and sat down beside me again. "So, I have never seen you here before."

"This is a regular hangout for me when I come visit." I replied.

"Well," he said as he pulled a baseball cap from his bag, "I just moved over here from St. Simons a couple of months ago. Jekyll seems to be the perfect place for me right now. I love the nature and the solitude. It's been exciting to see my art taking off but for the last year or so I can hardly go out for dinner without it turning into something about my work. I was getting approached to do gallery openings, charity events, and more. Not that I mind, but I wanted to have more privacy, and this was a perfect place for it. Plus, I need to be where my creative side can grow."

"I totally understand," I said. "That's why I love coming here. I started visiting about five years ago. I fell in love with the place, and I come back as much as I can. I don't know, it just seems special. As you might be able to tell, I am a dolphin fanatic."

"Are you one of those that love to go to the dolphin attractions?" he joked.

I looked at him seriously. "Actually, I can't stand those places. I feel like dolphins shouldn't live in captivity. I remember when I was about twelve years old, and my parents took me. I remember how upsetting it was for me. I can't explain it and you might think I am a bit out there, but sometimes I feel like I can communicate with them. When I saw them there, I felt like my heart was breaking in two. It was like I could look into their eyes and read their soul. Like they knew that they had to perform but even if they were born in captivity, they knew at a higher level they had been meant to live in the wild. So now do you think I am crazy?" I asked, trying to sound lighthearted.

"No, actually I think I can relate to it more than most folks. I have so many experiences with wildlife where I have seen deep into their eyes and thought that they know more than we do. It would be interesting if we could understand them better and communicate. That is the cool thing about dolphins. Their level of intelligence is amazing."

His words made me feel like I had met a kindred spirit. It made me feel good to know that he didn't think I was totally insane.

"Maybe you should go out on my boat with me sometime and we could go dolphin searching. It's much better than looking for them by the shore."

"Sounds fun."

He got this playful grin on his face. "Sounds like your schedule is open, so how about today?"

"Today?" I asked, shocked.

"Sure, why not." He nudged my shoulder. "Unless you have some schedule that you have to follow, but you are on vacation, right? I mean I'm not really a stranger since I am such good friends with Shelia."

He did have a point. My logical side was trying to convince myself that it might not be a good idea, but the adventurous girl screaming from inside told me to go for it. This trip was for me to rediscover myself, so now was the opportunity.

"Ok. I don't have a camera like yours, but I sure would love to take some pictures. You are welcome to walk back to my house with me and I can drive you to your car or wherever you need to go," I offered.

"I rode my bike here. How about I meet you at your house at ten-thirty and you can ride with me over to the boat dock?" he said.

"Sounds like a plan." I agreed. And an even better plan than what I suggested. I could get freshened up and pulled together.

We both got up and I shook the sand off the chair and stuffed my towel back in my backpack. "See you in a bit," he yelled as he walked away. And right before he was too far from me, he added, "You do have a swimsuit, right? I suggest you wear it. It's going to be a nice warm day."

Great. Now I had to think about going on a boat with someone I barely knew, finding an outfit and even worse, thinking about a bathing suit. I hadn't bought a new suit in over two years. It was a modest black and white two-piece. I hoped it didn't make me look too matronly or conservative. *Well Erin, how do you really want to look? Good question. He's just a friend taking me on an adventure. I'm officially married for goodness sake. I don't need to be thinking about him in any other way,* I reasoned. Although with his confidence and looks it would be difficult for any red-blooded American girl. *Cut yourself a break, Erin, and lighten up for once!*

I ran back to the house and jumped in the shower, washed my hair and blew it out with a round brush to accentuate my natural waves. I pulled back a portion of my hair into a barrette followed by some eyeliner, mascara, and lip gloss. I found a simple light blue sundress with silver flip flops and wore my swimsuit underneath. Right on time as he promised the doorbell rang. There he was dressed in navy swim trunks and a white T-shirt that clung to his muscles nicely.

"Ready to go?" he smiled.

"Sounds good!" I said, genuinely excited. The thought of seeing my dolphins up close from a boat made my heart race with anticipation. It was something I had only done a few times here. When I went with one of the local tour companies there were about twenty to thirty people on the boat. Those trips were awesome so I couldn't wait for this; my first time on a private cruise with no time clock and an open map.

He opened the passenger door so I could get in his jeep convertible. The top was off, so the wind could blow our hair. *Thank goodness I brought my ponytail holder.*

In less than ten minutes we arrived at the marina. Walking down the dock I was curious to know which boat was his. We came upon a boat that was older but totally renovated. "Wow," I said, "this is some boat."

"Thanks, I took the money from the sale of my house and some additional land in St. Simons to get the house over here and this boat. I still need to name her. It just hasn't come to me yet."

"You must have done pretty well on the sale." I tried to not sound too nosy or impressed.

"The house and land were my grandfather's and he left them to me. The set-up on this thing is great. I can stay overnight if I want. One of my dreams is to travel down the Intercoastal to the Keys and to some of the islands in the Caribbean."

He changed the subject and turned away. "Anyway, let me help you get situated and let's hit it. It's a perfect time as the tide is changing and sometimes the dolphins will get more active."

There was a briskness in the air, so I was glad when he offered me a blanket to throw over my lap. After pulling out of the slip he took a left heading toward the Atlantic Ocean. "Here, sit up here with me, so I can give you some history and show you the lay of the land."

I moved from the back sofas onto the deck then up the steps to the captain's area. The driver's seat was a bench seat. I sat to the left of him and felt his energy. *Has it been so long for me to feel a male energy like this?* And the answer was *yes.* Thinking back, I couldn't remember the last time Thom and I had a physical, much less an intimate connection. My mind drifted like the water bouncing off the sides of the boat. "You okay?" He asked, "You seem to be somewhere else."

"I'm fine. I was just thinking how long it's been since I have been out on the water," I lied. Then I thought about seeing my dolphins and pushed those thoughts aside.

"Okay, so let me give you some dolphin-searching pointers," he said. "See the front of the boat? We call that twelve o'clock. The boat acts like the base of a clock and your arm is like the dial. For example, if you see a dolphin over here, pointing ninety degrees to the right, that would be three o'clock."

"To the left is called Sharks Tooth beach. There is a trail you can hike on that takes you there, but I don't recommend you go alone. It is very woodsy and there could be snakes and spiders. If you go, you really should wear pants on the hike. otherwise, your legs will get cut up like crazy", he explained in tour guide fashion.

"So why do people go there?" I asked.

He answered. "Because people go to look for shark teeth that could be millions of years old. People have, you know, and for some it's like their obsession."

"Not me," I said, "Give me my dolphins every day and that's all I need," I said with a smile.

We passed the observation tower, St. Andrews picnic area on our left and we continued toward the ocean. He pointed out toward the water, "See all the islands? You can see Racoon Key, Cumberland Island, Little Cumberland Island, St. Simons, and of course, Jekyll.

"Did you know that John F. Kennedy, Jr. got married on Cumberland Island?" he asked.

"I heard that somewhere." I responded. "I have always wanted to go over there."

"I tell you what. I will take you over there one day and show you the horses. My friend is one of the caretakers of the inn."

"That would be cool." I said, "One of the paintings in Shelia's shop shows the horses," I reflected. "I loved how they were on the beach grazing."

He looked at me with his amber eyes. "I remember going out in my old boat one day. I had planned to beach on the island, but when I looked over, the horses were right on the beach, and I didn't have the heart to disturb them." I noticed the kindness in his voice. It was something that I had forgotten a man could have. He continued on in his reflection. "I was admiring them and then out of nowhere, a dolphin jumped in front of my boat. I guess she was playing with her pod. And that picture stuck in my mind. I went home and started painting it that day."

As we turned leftward, I saw my favorite beach spot. It was then I saw something come up out of the water. "Scott! Look, I think I saw one!" not realizing how excited my voice sounded. I kept my eyes peeled and sure enough there they were. A small pod of just three. Scott moved in closer with his boat.

"Look, there's more. We have them at eleven o'clock and two o'clock." Before I realized, there were at least fifteen dolphins surrounding our boat. "I have never seen this many at one time. Do you have a dolphin magnet in your pocket that I don't know about?" he teased.

His easy-going, open nature made me want to know more about him. I looked at him fully. His brown hair was blowing in the wind showing hints of gold flecks sprinkled in. Already tanned, I figured he stayed that way most of the year. His broad shoulders and tall physique made me wonder if he was ever into sports while growing up.

"What got you into painting?" I asked.

"It's funny how things change," he reflected. "I remember being able to draw as early as four or five. My mom and I would sit together. She would work with pencils and watercolors as a hobby. I must have some of her talent in me. But as I grew up my dad frowned upon it. I remember in eighth grade wanting to take an art class. My dad was not a fan. So, instead of fighting him I found a way to let out my creativity under his terms."

"I don't think parents know how much we do sometimes to please them," I said thinking back. "I would have done anything to get the approval of my mom. From my dad it came naturally."

"For me," he went on, "I think my father had a plan in his mind from the moment I was born. He started working for his dad in his teens, and he wanted me to follow in the family footsteps. My dad didn't go to college or get a degree. He grew up alongside my grandpa learning how to build houses and he wanted me to do some of the things he never did. Also, I think he was counting on me to do more for our family business. I put any dreams of art out of my mind and focused on what was expected of me. After growing up in Summerville, outside of Charleston all my life I got a full ride scholarship to the University of Michigan. It's top in the country for Architecture. After

I graduated, I moved back to Summerville and helped my dad grow the company."

"So what changed?" I probed. I looked in his eyes and saw the pain of remembering. It was a familiar ache I could relate to.

He turned his face away and stared out at the horizon. "It was almost four years ago now. Amy and I were living on Folly Beach."

"Who's Amy?" I interrupted. He had a distant and thoughtful look in his eyes.

"My wife." He took a long pull on the water bottle in his hand.

I didn't know what to say so I just decided to stay very quiet.

"We had been living there for only eight months. It was a place where we were going to build our family and create memories. It was perfect. It should have been. It took us three years to find it. I was working for our family company. She was an interior designer. That's how we met." His eyes had this faraway look about them. After a long pause, he continued. "It was a Thursday night and she had left a client's house around 9 pm. She had just called me to say she was sorry that she was late and had messed up our dinner plans. I was aggravated, so I was short with her on the phone." He sat there quietly. "The police said that they thought a deer, or some type of animal must have run out in front of her while she was driving, and she swerved to miss it. Her car flipped over in the median, and she died instantly."

I didn't know how to respond. My heart wanted to break for him and at the same time, I wanted to scream at the top of my lungs into the heavens and ask, *"What kind of God does this?"* I walked over to him and put a hand on his shoulder which led him to continue.

"Honestly, I turned into a machine for a while. A dead and empty shell on the inside, but folks thought I was operating fine. About seven months later I was moving her things out of the closet, and I just lost it. I couldn't find it in myself to want to go to work, leave the house or do anything. It was like the machine was out of gas and I had no way to fix it. One day my mom suggested that I go down to my grandfather's house in St. Simons. He had passed away a few months before and it was just sitting there. I packed up a duffel bag and came down."

He turned and looked into my eyes with such strength that I dared not turn my eyes from his. "I remember sitting on the beach early one morning and thinking about Amy. I used to doodle pictures for her and would hide them under her pillow or in her laptop bag so she would find them at work. It was a way to give a piece of myself to her that no one else had. I sat there in a fog but at the same time felt a processing I couldn't understand. I felt the ache within me release. I had been so angry at God. I couldn't understand why I had been punished when I thought I was a good person. In the middle of all that something birthed in me. And that's when I felt compelled to paint something that could show all my feelings. In my grandpa's house there was a sunroom where my mom used to paint and sketch. He had left it there all those years for when she would come down to visit. Lo and behold, I found pencils and chalks, so I picked one up. Before I knew it, it was five hours later, and my heart seemed to hurt a little bit less. It was like a medicine healing the invisible illness no one else could see. I feel more whole now than I ever have. In some weird way it's like Amy's passing has given me a new life that might have stayed dormant. I don't know if I am explaining that right," he said.

"How did you work through that anger with God? I just don't get it, that connection. I was raised where church was a series of formalities in a formal setting. I don't know if I really felt what some would call God. Well, maybe I have… I do remember something…" My voice faded out.

He picked up where I left off. "Well, you know that day that I showed up at my grandfather's place, next to the easel and art stuff was an open Bible. It had tons of tagged pages, and it was worn. I could tell by the handwriting on the page that it was his handwriting. The Bible was open to Isaiah forty, and I found myself reading:

> *He gives strength to the weary and increases the power*
> *of the weak. Even youths grow tired and weary, and*
> *young men stumble and fall; but those who hope in the*
> *The Lord will renew their strength. They will soar on wings*
> *like eagles; they will run and not grow weary, they will*
> *walk and not faint.*

It was like both my grandfather and God were telling me something. Erin, I wrote down those words on a piece of paper and put it in my wallet. I read those verses every single day to memorize them. Over those months I poured my time into studying his Bible with all of his notes and painting. Honestly, it has been a journey for me. I wonder how life takes its twists and turns. Out of the season of Amy's loss something came into me as a totally unexpected gift--- my painting. I feel like when I paint, I am showing how God looks at his creations, you know? One thing I can't explain is how God works, but I know that he showed up for me when I needed it. Painting healed such a part of me and at the same time it is my purpose, like my calling. I don't know if this makes any sense."

"You've explained it perfectly." I wanted to touch his hand but was afraid to. He brushed his hand through his hair and his gaze met mine. At that moment I knew we both felt a connection. Where it would lead, I didn't understand, as Scott knew nothing about the chapter I was in the middle of, but one thing I knew. I had a new friend… and that was worth its weight in gold.

CHAPTER 9

SCOTT

I decided to take a shower when I got home. With the water running over my body, I reflected on the day. *Why did you open up to her so much? You barely know her.*

Folks knew about Amy's death. But I never told anyone how I felt, especially not opening up about how my painting originated. It was too intimate to share with anyone. My painting allowed me to show my feelings without using words. Plus, my personal experience about how I found faith to move forward was something I hadn't even shared with my mom. I mean, she knew some things because I had asked her questions about Grandpa and his life. But I didn't go too deeply into the process.

I'm not sure what Erin unlocked in me. That first day I met her at the shop and then again on the beach, I knew there was something about her. When she had looked at me, I could see myself. I can't explain it, but I felt like she had a pain inside her like I once had.

I hoped that I could find out more about why she was on Jekyll. But she turned most of the conversation on me, distracting me from asking about her. How did that happen?

She was a good communicator, able to ask people questions, so they didn't ask her questions. She could wrap the entire conversation around their thoughts and their feelings. I didn't even realize she had done that until later.

I did learn about her connection with nature. We shared that. It was like every time I painted, I was connecting with something larger than myself, which put my problems and the scheme of the world into perspective.

I was drawn to her. It was different from my attraction to Amy in the beginning. Amy and I met through a mutual client, the Dubois family. They were a pillar in the James Island community and had known my father for years. When they looked at my architectural designs to turn their house into a postmodern contemporary, they hired me on the spot with one stipulation; that I work closely with their interior designer who happened to be Amy.

When you work that closely with someone creates a connection. That's what happened with Amy. She was so much more polished than I, with her southern girl charm. She smoothed out my edges.

But when I looked in Erin's eyes it was like our souls were connected by an invisible string making us move in sync. I didn't know what it meant, and it troubled me. I let the rain of water drench my head. *What does this feeling mean? Be careful Scott. Your heart can't handle another break.*

Maybe it could. But was I willing to risk it?

CHAPTER 10

ERIN

Yesterday was transformational for me. I don't know if it was the open water, the dolphins swimming or Scott sharing his story. But I found myself feeling refreshed with new hope that everything would work out in whatever way it needed to.

I had been here for a couple of weeks and knew the time had come to take the next step and face the things that lay ahead of me. I'd listened to Scott's account of his trying experience and heard how he had come through the other side of his pain. I desperately wanted this for myself too. *Erin, you can do this. You are stronger than you know.*

I am strong. I can do this. I will do this. All I have to do is dig down and do it. I can make anything happen that I need to. This pep talk was exactly what I needed to stop playing the victim and just get what was in front of me done.

While I had the courage, I picked up my cell phone and hit Thom's number. The first ring was hardly complete when he picked up and immediately burst out, "Geez, babe, I've been worried sick. I am so glad you finally called. I have been trying to reach you for days. I thought I would never hear from you. Laura is worried sick."

"Worried? Really? You didn't seem so worried the day I found you guys together." I sounded more hurt and fragile than I wanted to.

"Erin please. Just listen. Laura and I didn't plan this." Pausing, he continued, "It just happened," with a tone that made it excusable. *Did he honestly think that this was excusable?*

"How long has this been going on between the two of you?" I asked, afraid to know the answer.

"Erin, I don't think we should talk about this over the phone. When are you coming home? And where are you anyway?" He sounded aggravated, yet uncertain.

"I don't know when Thom, and honestly, I don't know what home is anymore. I just called to tell you that I am ok and that I will be in touch. Please don't call me and tell Laura the same. I need to figure things out on my own right now."

"Erin, come on we need to…" I didn't realize, but I had hung up the phone in the middle of his sentence. It didn't matter, anyway. I wrapped my arms around myself realizing that I was shaking from the inside out. Even still my adrenaline was running, but I had done what I set out to do.

I sat on the couch to steady myself. Was I shaking because I was sad or was it more fear of the unknown? *Oh my God. I don't love him anymore. How did this happen? When did this happen?* I realized I was praying. It had been so long since I had prayed. Maybe that's what got me into this mess. I had forgotten how to even pray anymore. Little by little, all my core pieces had been stuffed away like a closet filled with gunk. Time after time, until the things that are the necessities are not even locatable anymore.

In this moment of clarity I knew what I needed to do. I looked up the number to my dad's lawyer so that I could get a recommendation for a divorce attorney.

CHAPTER 11

ERIN

Even though I had relaxed some over the last couple of weeks, that call with Thom lingered in my mind. I didn't realize that my marriage was actually holding me back. Hearing his voice made me reflect on how I felt. When did I stop loving him? The question played in my mind. When you have been married to someone for nine years, you can't help but care about them. But how I felt wasn't how a wife should love her husband. Every part of me felt drained. I was battling between going to take a nap or pushing myself to go outside and get some air.

This intuitive voice kept reaching out to me. *Get this out of your heart Erin. Write it down.* This voice kept talking to me. Maybe that is why I picked up a journal from the island bookstore a couple of days ago. After working with Shelia at her shop, I had stopped into another gift shop to walk around. I spied a turquoise journal with a pretty ribbon bookmark attached. I hadn't written in years. Since high school really, but something made me pick it up and buy it.

With my beach chair, towel, journal and pen in my hand I walked to the end of where my steps hit the beach. I sank my toes into the soft sand. It made me think back through my memories to when things switched for me. I felt like a person who explains an out-of-body experience looking down at their own body. It was like a movie of someone else I was watching.

I looked out upon the water. The waves crashing up on the shore felt like a baptism of sorts, washing my hurt away. It was soothing.

I opened my journal and began to write.

March 30

It's been so long I don't even know how to start writing just for me. I can't explain why I bought this journal. I remember how my mom got so aggravated when she would see me carrying around my journal in high school. She couldn't understand that it was my release. It had become my best friend. It was the thing that never judged me for thinking or feeling a certain way. Songs and thoughts would pour out of me back then.

God, why did I stop writing? How did I get away from something that made me feel so complete? I don't know why I am even asking you. You probably don't even care or know me anymore, do you? Or maybe you don't even exist. All the religious stuff is well just that: stuff. Wow. I'm sorry. I know you really exist, in some form, anyway. I don't know why I buried that away the morning that dad passed away. I don't even want to write it down right now. It's just too much.

So why am I talking to you? Maybe I am hoping that you are there. I remember my grandma always praying. Bessie. I never understood how she could be on her knees for hours just praying. When I was about six or maybe seven, I walked in the hallway and in her bedroom, I could see her praying, asking to keep His hand on my dad. His hand? I totally couldn't get that. Did God have a hand? I had never seen it before. How funny we as kids take things so literally. She was going to town, too. Just praying like a warrior, using the bed to lean against, like it was her war field or something. My mom always said Grandma Bess was too eccentric for her taste. I don't know if they ever saw eye to eye on that kind of stuff. It could have been because Dad's side of the family was old school. You know, country. Shoot, one time as a kid I tried to figure out our family tree. Our family went so far back between the western areas of North Carolina and the Virginias, I couldn't even find paperwork on some of our family. I don't know if it was because the Virginia's handle split into their own states, or if back then things just weren't documented. All I know is that my dad's side of the family went back a long way. Praying was like eating. You just did it every day and over every single thing. I remember Grandma praying over hulling walnuts with the tips of her fingers all black. She would be picking the muscadine grapes off the vine with me and praying over that too. "Thank you, Jesus, for giving us these big ole' grapes" she'd say in her Appalachian accent. Now that I think about it, she would turn her prayers into little songs walking around the house or just swinging on that big front porch of hers. She was humble from her roots even though Grandpa had gone to college with all his savings from working on farms and mowing lawns growing up. He definitely passed his talent for business and numbers down to my dad, that's for sure.

Then there was my mom's side of the family which was just different. I don't know if they really believed in God or not. They saw all the fear, fighting, and hiding that took place in Denmark when Hitler was in power. I remember my MorMor telling me about their family-run bakery and her brother who worked underground to steal weapons from the Germans so he could get them into the hands of the Danish people for protection. FarMor, my grandpa, was bitter for years and who could blame him. When he was little, his dad was taken off to a concentration camp where he died of tuberculosis. He would say that God and religion were the reason for all these "damn wars." He believed in making it on his own regardless of any God upstairs. And he did. He was sponsored by a family to come to America with less than ten dollars in his pocket, then he joined the Navy. After he got here, he proposed to my grandma, and they started their life.

Wow, I never considered until just now, maybe that is why my mom seemed to be so driven. Maybe that was just all she knew. Maybe that is why she didn't understand me back then. Yeah. Now that I think about it, when we visited my mom's side of the family, I knew there would be no whining allowed. It was 'suck it up and get through it' mode. I wonder if that is why I felt mom never understood me. Shoot, I don't know. I do have some of that in me, too. Maybe more than I want to admit. But on the other hand, I have this piece of me I buried somewhere along the way. Does that just happen?

I think it was college. I got so wrapped up in doing what I needed to be doing, there was no time to daydream anymore. I needed to get things done. I remember the day Mom and Dad dropped me off at college. It was like she was glad I was leaving home. I remember thinking, well if that is how you feel then I will never be dependent on you again. I will make my own way, Mom. I don't need your approval anymore.

Wow. Did my anger at her make me so determined to achieve and not fail? Man, I have some issues. Yeah, it's about time I started admitting it.

UGGGHHH. I feel so lost. What am I supposed to do now? I feel so alone. Like I have been doing all these things for people so that I can feel… but feel what, Erin? Significance? Maybe that is what has caused all this. Maybe it's me. Did I not give Thom what he needed?

I don't even know what I need to give myself. So, God, if you are listening, please help me find my way. I don't know how to find my way anymore. I am scared. Maybe you are what gave me the strength to call Thom this morning. I honestly don't know where that came from. But I think you gave me that strength when I lost Dad and the baby and now you are back again giving me this strength when I don't have it within myself to carry on. I guess I need to say I'm sorry. Because looking back, I have just called on you when times were tough, like with my dad and the baby. And now look, here I am again. So, I'm sorry. It's pretty selfish of me thinking that I just call on you and you come runnin'. Ha! That sounds exactly what grandma Bess would tell me if she were here. I miss her. I should have told her I loved her more. God, can you tell her that for me?

Through the times and through the years

You've been the one to calm my fears…

So true. I drifted away from church and how I was raised. As an adult and especially in college, I wasn't a consistent church-going girl. But after everything I went through over the last two years, I knew there was some higher power. I couldn't explain it. I had to believe that there was some power helping me on my journey.

That is why I am writing. It's my plea. So, God, if you're really listening, I am asking right now to give me strength and please show me what I am supposed to do. I know there is an answer, so please show me.

I closed my journal, wiping the tears from my eyes. I looked out over the waves and spied one fin come up. It was a single dolphin. *I thought they swam in pods.* How weird. It was a sign. A sign that although it might look like I am alone I am really not.

I got up from my chair and walked closer to the water's edge. It was like she was swimming directly toward the beach. It felt like she was aware her energy was transferring to me; I could actually feel it. I knew to keep my distance from wild dolphins. But it didn't stop her from coming in closer and closer to the shore. As I continued to watch, I saw her come higher up out of the water and show her belly, a soft, bright pink. I studied somewhere that a pink belly indicated that she was pregnant. "Wow girl. You are in the phase of creating a new chapter in your life too, huh?" I said aloud pretending she could hear me.

As quickly as she had come to visit, she turned back out toward the open water, most likely to connect with her pod. She was my sign; my sign to remember that even though I couldn't see it in front of me, things would work out. Maybe, just maybe, God heard my prayer after all.

CHAPTER 12

SOPHIA

I had just finished lunch with my realtor friend Diane, when my phone rang. Erin's name came up on the screen.

"Hello?"

"Hi mom, it's me. I just wanted to check in and say hi."

It was so good to hear her voice. But I didn't want to appear too anxious to ask her questions and scare her off the phone. "Darling, it is so great to hear from you. Are you having a good time?" I asked lightly.

"It's good to be down here," she said. "I have been spending a lot of time on the beach and helping my friend with her shop. The other day I went out on a boat and got to see a ton of dolphins. It was breath-taking." Even though it sounded like she wanted to talk, her voice sounded guarded.

Since she was about ten years old, Erin had a love affair with dolphins. Matthew and I took her to Hilton Head for vacation. We took a private tour on a skiff boat. The captain took us through the creeks and marshes that eventually fed into the ocean. She was mesmerized when she saw dolphins come right up to the boat. It was an interesting sight to see. It was like they had a spiritual connection with her. Even the boat captain couldn't believe how they stayed at our boat for so long. Erin placed her hand over the side of the boat and a dolphin brought his nose to her hand and she stroked him. I never saw anything like that. Even though Matthew and I also put our hands over the side, they only allowed her to touch them. From then on, it was as if she was obsessed with them.

She read constantly about their habits, livelihood and rituals. She had posters up on her wall for the longest time.

"That's wonderful darling. When are you heading back to Charlotte?"

"Well, that is why I am calling. I don't want to go into all the details right now, Mom. But I thought you should know, because I don't want you talking to Thom. I have filed for divorce. I talked to one of dad's friends. You remember Dennis Kirsch, right? Well, he is handling it. There may be some ways we can expedite the process and get it done fairly quickly. I am all in on that."

I was quiet for what seemed to be like an eternity. I needed to be careful. Our relationship was strained enough, and I didn't want to shut down our communication. "Have you told Laura yet? What did she say about it?"

"Mom. Please. I don't need this third degree." She sounded harsh.

"I'm sorry." I said quietly, afraid to say much else. "I just meant she is your best friend. You never keep any secrets from each other."

"Well maybe I should just let the cat out of the bag. No use beating around the bush, because after I say it, I don't want to talk about it. Seriously, Mom." Erin's tone was firm. "I found Thom and Laura in bed together. I don't know how long it has been going on. The day I found out, I got a place down here to just clear my head. Work organized my schedule and well, it is what it is." You could hear a pin drop. She was definitely not ready to elaborate, and I couldn't blame her. My anger was welling up just thinking about it. *Her best friend? If best friends could do this, who needed enemies?*

"WHAT? Oh Erin, I don't even know what to say. Is there anything I can do for you?"

"Not right now." she said, decisively. "Well, except, please don't take any calls from Laura or Thom, ok? I would really like you to honor that."

"Sure darling, of course I will. I know things have happened, but I don't want you to think that I am not here for you. Please call me. I love you. You know I would do anything for you."

Erin's voice cracked. "Thanks Mom. I needed to hear that. I will give you an update soon," then she hung up.

When I put down the phone, I pondered what she told me. I wished we could talk like other mothers and daughters. *I don't know what that even looks like.* Somehow, over time she had made her own opinions about me. I am sure I didn't help the situation. Starting my career when she was so young was probably hard on her. Her other friends had moms that stayed at home, came to every school party and volunteered on the field trips. Me, on the other hand, I was working. It's amazing what you do when fear and love become mixed together. That is what drove me, but I never told her the whole story. There just never seemed to be a time or a need to talk about it.

Matthew's illness taught me to be the strong one. He didn't need to be worried about me, so I learned to hide my feelings. I became the master of disguising what I really felt. Before I knew it, it had become a habit. When Erin would show her teenage sass, I would put on my smile and act like it didn't bother me. I didn't want to show my pain. I remember the day Matthew and I drove her to Duke to get her settled in the dorm for her first year of school. I didn't want her to see how sad I was to see her leave. I was so good at pushing emotions down; it was easier to do than bringing them to the surface.

When she got pregnant last year, I thought we could have a fresh start. I started buying her gifts for the nursery even though she was only five or six weeks along. It was like something we could bond over. But when she lost the baby, I felt like she pulled even further away from me. It was like she didn't want to face me because she didn't want to have a conversation about it.

If there was one thing I could change, I'd love a 'do over' with Erin. Show her how much I admired her, accepted her, and loved her with all my heart. No matter what. I hoped to God I would get that chance.

CHAPTER 13

ERIN

The days were running away from me. I couldn't believe my rental lease would be up soon and I had no desire to return home. Dialing the office, Don picked up quickly. "Hey Don, how are you?"

"Great Erin, but we are sure missing you," he said.

"Is everything running ok?" I asked, worried.

"Things are going well," he said. "Kim is running things. You trained her well. But she is not you. You are the heartbeat behind a lot of this now."

A weird twinge hit my stomach, but I pushed through. "That's great to hear." *Or is it anymore?* "I know that this might be asking a lot, but I hope you are willing to help. I know I'm due back in a few weeks. I was wondering if I could have another month off without pay. I know it might be an inconvenience. I could use the time to take care of some personal things. That is, if the team can get along without me."

"Erin, I need you, but I get it. You need time. After all these years I can't judge that," he said. "I have an idea. The hotel down there is looking to expand their marketing and advertising campaign with us.

They're building another hotel on Saint Simons." He kept going in his fast-paced business mode. "They've asked us to put together an offline strategy, social media campaign, and some website additions to build their database. Would you consider being a liaison for us as the voice of the project? You are down there experiencing the area in its true form. If anyone can relate to why folks would want to visit, it's you. That's the type of emotion and connection we need with this fresh campaign. It's not a full-time schedule, probably fifteen-to-twenty hours a week at most, but I'm willing to keep you on salary, if you can oversee it. This is a huge contract for us. I believe it will open up doors to other luxury hotels. Are you up for that? We don't have to schedule a meeting until two weeks from now, so that gives you some more time before jumping back on the horse," he said with a laugh.

How could I say no to that? I could stay here, get paid and have the time I wanted. "Sounds great, Don and thank you for the opportunity. I really appreciate it." A part of me felt a concerned tug that I should take some more time for myself, but this was an offer I couldn't refuse.

"You know Erin, I'm pretty sure we could arrange for you to stay at the hotel on the island if you want. Do you want me to look into that?"

"Let me think about that, Don. I do like where I am staying right now. I'm not sure if I will need to change where I am staying." After hanging up I thought about Don's offer. Perhaps this would provide a distraction from thinking about what my life was going to be like without Thom.

Now I needed to see what options were available on my rental. Before going to Shelia's shop, I stopped off at Ocean Realty. As I expected, Jack was sitting at his desk. His warm eyes and smile radiated when I walked in the door. Jack owned a realty company in Tennessee and settled here after his wife retired from teaching. He was close to the age that my dad would have been, and it felt good to have someone that I felt genuinely cared about me. He came out from behind his desk to give me a warm hug. "Hey there Kiddo! How are you enjoying the island?"

"It's great Jack. In fact, I wanted to see if you could call the owners to see if I could extend my stay through Memorial Day. I know you mentioned that the sellers come back every summer, but I just arranged a longer stay. Could you work that out for me?"

"Sure thing," he replied with a huge grin. "I don't think that will be a problem. It's early enough before it gets too busy down here for the summer. I'll give them a call this morning. And little lady, it looks like the island is getting to you. You seem much better since that first day you picked up the keys. I am so glad. And, don't you forget, Lisa and I would love to have you over for dinner anytime. The door is always open at our house."

"Thanks so much!" They were a wonderful older couple, and it felt nice to be looked after. "Just let me know what I need to do or sign, and I will stop back by." I said my goodbyes and headed toward Shelia's.

When I walked in the door of the shop, I found Shelia on a ladder hanging a wind chime from the ceiling. She turned around, her typical huge smile showing those white teeth, "Hey girl! It's been a while since I saw you! I was just about ready to come over to your place and kidnap you for a girls' night out. What's up?"

"Sorry about that. I have been a bit busy taking care of some things the last few days. It looks like I will be here through the end of May now. My boss is putting me on a special project that will start in a couple of weeks for one of our clients down here."

"Wow! That's awesome! Scott stopped in yesterday and told me that you guys went out on the boat together. I think he will likes you, Erin. Anything you want to tell me?"

"Not much," hoping I was good at concealing my real thoughts, "I don't want to go there, Shelia. I don't know if it's right to be interested in anyone when I am not officially divorced yet, you know? I am focused on closing the marriage chapter in my life. I don't feel Scott is something that should be in the middle of all this. Speaking of which, I called my attorney, and he drew up the papers and is sending them. Who knows, Thom might have already gotten them. He says that there are some things that can move the divorce process along that can actually settle this quicker than normal. Something about the other apartment he owns in uptown being in the second-year lease. I don't want to get into all that drama. Honestly, the lawyer conversations drive me a bit insane. All I know is my decision is made. My line in the sand is drawn and I am done."

She looked at me with concerned eyes, "You don't waste any time, do you? Are you sure about this?"

"I can't explain it, but I think this is what I have needed to do for a long time. I knew it, but I pushed it away. Even when my dad was sick, I knew."

"That long?" she asked.

"Yeah. I know, right? I thought I could save it. I thought if we had a family, our relationship would turn a corner and well, here we are. What happened a few weeks ago was the catalyst to get me unstuck, I think. Does that make sense?"

"It does," she said, hugging me close. "I am so sorry you have gone through so much, sweetie. You never told me. You always looked so pulled together every time I saw you, like you were living the perfect life or something. I'm proud of you and want you to know that I am here for you and sincerely I have been praying for you. Just put your trust in God and I know He will direct your path. He did it for me years ago."

"You had things years ago?" I ask. "You never mentioned it."

"Yes, and I came through the other side with much greater opportunities that would have never presented themselves. That is why I know that new beginnings are ready for the taking. Speaking of new beginnings," she said with a mischievous smile, "I had a date with a neat guy last night. I was just getting ready to call you with the details."

"I want to hear about that for sure. But first I have to ask, did the dolphin painting of Scott's sell yet? I don't see it."

"It's in the room to the right," she pointed and started walking there so I followed her. "The one of 'Sapelo' sold to that couple I had mentioned. I suspect it won't be long before this one is gone," she said as she looked up at my painting. I heard my voice whisper to me, *just relax. If the painting is meant to be, it will be. Let things go. You can't control everything or plan everything in your life. Look where that has gotten you.* Sometimes I wish that voice would shut up, but for once it was right. Up until now I had tried to control things, and it seemed the harder I held on, the more pain and loss it caused.

When I looked into the dolphin's eyes in the painting, she seemed to be smiling at me; as if she was letting me know that I was on the right path to something great, but I just had no idea what. I was going to hold on to that; I had to.

"Okay, do tell me about that date!" I loved the way she was so carefree. *I need to hang with this girl more often.* She definitely had a joy in her that I longed for.

CHAPTER 14

SCOTT

The last several days kept me busy.

Being out with Erin that day on the beach inspired me. Those pictures I took of her haunted me until I had no choice but to pick up my paintbrush and start painting her. Since I'd begun painting, I'd only created natural landscapes and animals. Not that I couldn't paint something else. I hadn't felt compelled to do so. Once I put the paint to the canvas, I couldn't stop myself.

I couldn't get that morning out of my mind as I painted. Her face was imprinted in my mind, sitting on the beach with her knees pressed up against her chest, her chin perched on her hands. When she had looked at me in those moments there seemed to be a longing, a wishful dreaming behind her eyes. There was also this intent of searching for something; like she didn't even know what she was looking for. In the distance dolphin fins glided above the water.

You need to call her and tell her about the painting.

I didn't know if it was the right time to do that, but I knew that I wanted to see her, so I dialed the number.

CHAPTER 15

ERIN

The phone rang as I was walking in the door, back from the grocery store. "Hello?" I said, a bit out of breath from carrying the bags.

"Am I catching you at a bad time?" It was great to hear Scott's voice and at the same time gave my stomach a flip-flop.

"No, not at all," I said. "I just got home. I went to see Shelia and then drove over to Brunswick to do some shopping. My fridge was in major need of a fill up and the island store has little to choose from in comparison to across the bridge."

"I know what you mean. I try to make it a pit stop when I am over there running errands or doing business. I was thinking about you and wanted to say, "hey". I haven't talked to you in a few days because I went up to Savannah to meet with a gallery owner. On top of that, I've been painting and sometimes the time gets away from me."

"What are you painting?" I was curious.

"Well, it's something that I would like to talk to you about. Can we meet for dinner tonight? I was thinking we could go to the Bistro Restaurant up the road."

"Dinner sounds great, but I'll tell you what, I have been dying to make a home cooked meal and haven't had company yet. What do you think about coming over and letting me do that? It would give me a chance to thank you properly for taking me out on the boat the other day."

"Sounds good. What time?"

"How about seven?"

"It's a date," he said.

CHAPTER 16

ERIN

Before I could correct him that this was clearly not a date, he hung up. It was at that moment that I realized he might be interested in me. He didn't know the baggage attached to my hip.

Oh no, a date? I just realized that he knew nothing about me. I hadn't told him anything about why I was here. That day I had diverted my story and gotten him talking about his life. He didn't even know about Thom, unless Shelia had told him. But I highly doubt she had. She wasn't the type. So, this was going to be interesting. Yes, my divorce papers were underway. But was it really appropriate to lead him on thinking that this could be a date? My logical brain processed it, but I am not sure if my emotions were falling in line.

I had to find a way to tell him. My stomach felt icky all of a sudden. Pushing it down, I refocused.

I quickly put the groceries away. It was three o'clock. Great, I have four hours to figure out what I'm cooking for dinner. I just got back from the store and now I had no idea what to cook. What's with that!

I decided to wing it since I had no clue what he even liked. Steaks were usually a hit with men, paired with homemade mashed potatoes and a green salad. "I got this," I said out loud, determined to convince myself.

I took two filets out of the fridge along with fresh garlic, teriyaki sauce, olive oil, and some salt and pepper. In the bowl, I combined the ingredients, then poured it into a zip-lock bag with the steaks to marinate. Since I had a while before dinner, I grabbed my beach chair, journal and pen and hit the beach to write. I knew it was my therapy, and I felt like it might be good to get things out of my head and heart before Scott came over. I wanted to make sure I didn't have anything built up that might come spilling out to him.

April 18, Thursday

Scott is coming over for dinner tonight. He called and asked if I wanted to grab dinner and before I knew it, I was inviting him over to my house.

It's different going out in public versus being here at my place. Plus, I can't remember how long it's been since I have cooked for someone besides Thom. And even Thom, I can't remember the last time…

Speaking of Thom, I can't believe everything I have done over the last few weeks since all this began. I don't even know what to put as a name to this mess. I hired the attorney. At least things are underway. I know it is the right thing to do. I don't have it in me to be angry right now or to be sad. I have been sad for too long. Isn't it weird when you look back on things, you realize it?

Ok, who am I kidding? Of course, I am sad. How could I not be? I realize the dream I had concocted in my mind, from when we first fell in love, is dead. Another thing dead. I remember in his last few weeks Dad would ask me to read his favorite Bible passages to him. Looking back, I wish I had asked him why he wanted those certain ones. One of them that seemed to be stuck in my brain was, "In everything give thanks for this is the will of God in Christ Jesus concerning you." He had me memorize it when I was just a kid. (I Thessalonians 5:18)

Now seeing all that has happened I just don't get it. Really? Everything? I don't even get that. How could bad things be His will? Seriously?

I remember that Saturday before he passed. He was lying in bed at home. I was sitting by his side holding his hand. He looked at me and said, "Honey, you look so sad. Life is too short. I want you to promise me that you will find your happiness again. I haven't seen your smile, your real smile, in so long."

"I know Daddy," I told him. "I'm trying and I promise. I love you, Dad."

Four days later he was gone.

When had my troubles with Thom started? How had it gotten to that place of never turning back?

I believe it started when my dad's cancer was progressing. I remember coming home one night after a long drive back from Winston-Salem. I had been at the hospital with my dad. Thom seemed so distant and aggravated that I had been gone and not back in time for dinner. "Are you mad at me? What's wrong?" I asked him. I didn't want him upset, but I truly hoped he understood what I needed to do.

"I know your dad is important Erin, but do you have to be at practically every treatment for him? What about us? You weren't here for the dinner meeting with my boss, and this is important for my career. They're considering me for a partner in the firm and your presence is a big piece for me. I need you too, you know."

For as long as I could remember he never understood the closeness between me and my father. The first couple of years of marriage it wasn't an issue. I was a typical young woman in my twenties focused purely on Thom and my career while my parents took a back seat.

I remember the day it changed. My mom called from the doctor's, telling me that I needed to come home. There was something they needed to tell me. Stage four lung cancer. I could hardly comprehend it. He didn't even smoke. When my dad had colon cancer, I was too young to know and understand. But now, it hit me with a wave of uncertainty. I was always the type that I could find a way to make things happen, but this was totally out of my control. How was I supposed to fix this? I knew I couldn't control the cancer but by God, I could control my actions. I was going to be with my dad every step of the way, just like he was for me growing up.

He needed me and I needed to be there for him. Even though my mom looked like she was holding it together pretty well; there were times that I could see her turn away with tear-filled eyes and her hands shaking while signing paperwork. It was enough to know that I needed to be there. Thom was always so self-sufficient. He played golf every Tuesday and Friday afternoon; followed by the never-ending Friday evening cocktails where it was pretty much understood the wives weren't invited. He didn't need me the way my dad did. When you realize the clock is ticking on life, you notice it.

That year Thom and I continued to drift apart. Before I knew it, we were living separate lives. In the beginning, he criticized me for not being there for him. He said that my father and my career were more important than him. Was that true? It wasn't, but I didn't know how to juggle all the balls in the air. I had to be there for my dad, and I had to keep my career, so didn't something have to give? I tried… I really tried to do it all. I guess it just wasn't enough…

I don't know how it happened, but eventually we both just stopped arguing and settled into our own quiet existence.

When Dad died, Thom went through the motions of helping me and my mom. But I could feel the distance between us. I remember sitting next to him at the funeral and feeling all alone.

When I got pregnant seven months later, I thought it was our chance at a new beginning. That loss was just as bad, maybe even worse in some ways. And now another beginning seems to be in front of me – I have to start all over again. It's just not how I saw life unfolding. There are so many twists and turns, like me serving dinner tonight to someone that seems to read my mind… Speaking of that, I better get ready…

I closed my journal, packed up my things and walked the trail back to my house to get ready.

CHAPTER 17

SCOTT

I pulled into her driveway about five minutes late, trying not to appear overly anxious to see her. Deep down, I couldn't wait. The energy she gave off was intoxicating to me. It made me crave more time around her. I didn't have any clue about her back story. Shelia was tight-lipped and Erin was like a vault. Ever since she sat with me that morning on the beach and I saw her eyes light up, I knew there had to be more than what she was letting on. When she looked at the dolphins, I sensed a hurt deep inside her that made me want to protect her in some way.

She left the front door open, so I was able to see inside the house and hear the music. After a quick knock, she appeared. Her smile warmed me from the inside out. "Hey; perfect timing, I was just going to open some wine. Would you like some?"

"That sounds great." I couldn't help but look at her from top to bottom. Her V-neck blue lightweight sweater hugged her in all the right places. It made her eyes sparkle like blue topaz. Her auburn hair was streaked with hints of caramel and blond wisps that cascaded down her back. It made me want to reach out and run my hands through it to touch the different variations of color. But that would be something I would need to resist. For now, anyway.

"Can you open this bottle for me?" she asked. "Here is the wine opener." As I went to take it from her hands our fingers brushed against each other, and I felt the chemistry pass between us. "While you do that, I will work on mixing up the salad. I hope you like steak. Are you open to helping with the grilling?"

"Sounds great." I couldn't take my eyes off her, but I knew that I couldn't tell her. Shelia had mentioned casually about her leaving Charlotte in a rush. I wasn't sure what was going on there and I wanted her to trust me.

"Hey, I love this piano." I pulled out the seat, opened the lid and grazed my fingers across the keys. "I always wanted to play, but it wasn't in the cards for me. How about you?" The look in her eyes said something more than her voice wanted to. I could tell, but I just stayed quiet to see what she would say.

"I took lessons most of my childhood," she said. "My mom wanted me to learn classical. She and I butted heads over it because I was always making up my own melodies and writing a lot of my own music. By the time I hit the end of my junior year in high school, I just stopped. I got tired of the constant aggravation over it with her. She never really understood my love of creating my own music. It was like she just wanted me to learn the technical fundamentals so it would make me marketable for college or something. For me, music was a way to express myself. The more she pushed me to play what she wanted, the more resentful I got. I just didn't want to feel that anymore. So, I stopped. After a while it just got easier for me to ignore the pull. It's funny how you can phase something out of your life that was once so important to you."

I looked into her eyes, and I understood how she felt. I also knew that music was what was going to heal whatever she was going through.

"Do you remember how to play? I would love to hear you."

She looked at me with those baby blues. "I don't know… I haven't played in a long while. I wonder if I even know how anymore."

"Maybe it's like riding a bike."

"How about that wine?" The blush in her cheeks lit up her eyes even more. I got up from the piano and closed the lid. "How about I help you with the salad and then turn on the grill for us? By any chance do you have any water? I gave up drinking after Amy…"

"Oh sure!" She blushed. "Let's see, I have bottled water, some diet soda and oh, I almost forgot – homemade sweet tea! Can you believe that? I figured down here in Georgia I better figure out how to make some real tea." She laughed.

"That would be great. It's probably my favorite thing to drink even though it's probably not the healthiest thing." Wow, I loved the way she smiled at me. I was getting addicted to that face.

"So," I felt compelled to ask, "You know a lot about me, but I still don't know enough about you. What brought you down here to Jekyll?"

"Well, I guess you could say I am starting a new chapter in my life. This is the place for me to do it and see what new perspective I gain."

"Have you ever been married?"

A sad expression crossed her face for a brief moment. "Yes. I am in the middle of a divorce." She didn't offer more but I could see a pain from behind her eyes making me think, *did she still love him?*

I changed the subject. "So, let's get that grill warmed up. I am looking forward to a great steak. It's been a while. Just tell me what I need to do."

"Well, I wish I could tell you how to turn that baby on," she pointed to the grill with a laugh, "but I am not exactly a grill master. The only thing I can tell is it's a gas grill."

"No problem. Leave it to me, Let's go out on the patio and get it going." Grabbing our drinks, we headed outside to check out the grill. She had the table decorated with a candle centerpiece, outside dishes, silverware, and placemats all set up.

"It's such a beautiful night, I thought we could sit outside," she said. "It's supposed to be a great night to see the stars and the moon. Next Thursday it will be a full one."

"Maybe if we feel up to it, we could check out the beach after dinner," I offered, hoping that she would say yes.

"Sure, it sounds like a perfect plan."

"How do you like your steak?" I asked.

"Medium for me, please," she said casually.

"I tell you what, why don't you sit back and relax, since you've done all this planning, and I will take care of this."

"A man after my own heart."

Well, that was definitely the truth.

CHAPTER 18

ERIN

During dinner we talked about everything ranging from our favorite meal to our favorite sports. I couldn't remember the last time I had such a connection with someone like I had with Scott.

He was like a paradox. On one hand, he made me feel so comfortable and at ease in my own skin. On the other hand, when I looked at him or we would brush against each other, there was this electricity that I couldn't relate to. It was a feeling I never had before. Feeling on edge with this emotion and at the same time feeling comfortable was weird. I enjoyed it actually, and that also scared me a bit, that my life could change on a dime. But right now, it wasn't the time to dwell on it, here in front of him.

"Wow, that was such a great meal," he said.

"I can't take all the credit," I replied. "The steaks were perfect. Maybe you missed your real calling. You could travel the country doing those Barbeque contests." I teased.

His laugh warmed me. "Well, I wouldn't go that far, but I am pretty comfy with the grill. I make some great ribs too."

"Yum. I'll have to try that sometime."

"Well, we'll just need to make that happen then," he said sincerely.

Of course my little inner voice would have to chime in, *where is this going? I don't know, but I am going to just let it be.* We carried our dishes from the patio into the kitchen.

"Let me help clean up," he said.

"You don't have to do that. You're my guest."

"I want to," he said with his gorgeous smile.

"You have a great smile." I meant it, but once it was out of my mouth, I felt like a college girl trying to pick up a guy.

"I got it from my grandma who passed away a few years back. She told me a saying when I was a kid and it's always stayed with me. 'Smile and it will come back to you."

"I love that." I felt the warmth inside as I said it.

We stood side by side, rinsing the dishes and loading them into the dishwasher. It felt good to have a man beside me, helping me. It made me feel like I was something special and that home meant as much to him as me. I realized now, just shy of thirty-five, that I was discovering what a real man was. Even though my dad had shown that example to me, I didn't comprehend it until this exact moment.

"How about we check out that sky?" Scott asked.

"Sure, let me just grab a jacket since it's a bit cool."

"That's a good idea," he said. "I have one out in my jeep and I think I might have some binoculars. Let me go get them." As he went out, I grabbed my jacket, a blanket, and a red flashlight even though it wasn't officially turtle season.

I met him outside by his jeep and we walked side by side down the hidden grassy path to the beach. The wind was calm, and the crashing waves were singing in unison. The quarter moon complimented the multitude of stars shining above. It made me think about what my dad told me when I was a little girl after Sunday School. "Sweet pea, anytime you wonder if there is a God looking over you just look up. He made all of this; and he made you just like the stars, to shine brightly and give light." I would have forgotten it if he had just said it once. But through the years he would always remind me and then finish it with, "How dare you not shine." It would always come when I was questioning myself or worried that I wasn't good enough to try something new; afraid I would fail. The thought of him sent shivers up my arm. A breeze brushed the wisps of my bangs.

"You look a little cold," he said, with concern in his voice. "I brought this sweatshirt just in case. It might be big though. Do you want it?"

"Yeah. That would be awesome." I slid it over my head and looked down to read the yellow word MICHIGAN on the chest area. *Of course, it would say Michigan.* I thought with a girlish smile.

"Let's put the blanket down on the sand and walk a bit. The blanket should be fine since the tide is going back out," he said.

He naturally took my hand in his. A shot of electricity surged through my body. It felt right. Like a perfect fit. My logic was trying to battle with my heart saying that it was too soon. There was no way I wanted to be grouped into the caliber of what Thom and Laura had done while Thom and I were married. Here I was entering uncharted territory without a map. My heart enjoyed the comfort I felt, though. I felt that holding my hand wasn't disrespectful. It was like he was just showing me that I wasn't alone, and I was understood. I knew there was this attraction and at the same time I knew that he was a gentleman at heart. My heart swelled with appreciation. This was the type of man my dad tried to explain to me all those years ago. But as a young woman I hadn't understood. Until now.

We stopped to study the sky and its vastness. It was so clear that the stars leapt out from the darkness.

"There is supposed to be a meteor shower in a few weeks. I am going to go out that night, if you are interested. I have a telescope." He said quietly as he turned and faced me in the darkness.

I couldn't help myself but to say, "I'd like that a lot."

It was then as his lips lightly brushed mine that I knew Scott was more than a transition or a rebound. This was real. He was real.

CHAPTER 19

SCOTT

Her kiss was something I had wanted for days. That's why I took a break from seeing her or inviting her along on my Savannah trip. Even though we just met, I felt this gravitational pull to her. I knew I needed to take it slow but seeing her in the moonlight, staring up at me with those beautiful eyes and with the sound of the waves crashing around us was too irresistible. I sure didn't know how to handle this. With her in the middle of a divorce I didn't understand what was politically correct either. I didn't know how long she would be here, but I knew one thing. I had to follow my instincts. The pain in my past had taught me that lesson. This was possibly a second chance at love and even though it might be painful to lose again, I had to take this chance.

I knew logically this could be dangerous, but something larger seemed to push me forward.

When I brushed a strand of her hair from her face she smiled back with smoldering eyes. Like two angels on my shoulder each telling me different things, a voice came, "You have to take this slow Scott… don't rush this and lose everything." I had to get control of my mind and my body. I had to get off this treacherous terrain and change course. But at that moment, I couldn't find a way. As she looked up at me, I leaned into her and brushed her warm lips against mine. When we broke from the kiss, she rested her head on my chest as my arms enclosed around her frame.

It felt so natural that I lost track of time standing there feeling the sand beneath my toes. It was like we were not sure what to say or if we should say anything at all.

After a few moments of quiet, I looked down at her. "I wish I could read her mind." Her eyes gave her away. I could see that we were both feeling something deeper than we had expected.

"So, what are you up to this weekend?"

"Shelia and I discussed hanging out here or possibly heading down to St. Augustine for a couple of days." she said looking like she wasn't really sure.

"You'll like St. Augustine," I said. "I have some art down there too. It's a neat town."

"What about you?"

"I have to go up to Charleston tomorrow and stay through Sunday. There is an art festival there and my work is being featured in one of the galleries on Broad Street. My agent wants me there to meet people looking at my art tomorrow and Saturday night. It's not my favorite thing to do, but it's necessary. People are curious to meet the artist behind the work, especially if they're collectors."

Invite her to come with you Scott. No… I better not. It's too soon. Too fast. I want to but I better not. I guess I could ask my college friend Steven, who had been a pastor for sixteen years. Maybe I was afraid of the advice he'd give me.

"It's getting late," she said lightly. "We should probably turn back."

I was dying to take her hand but felt reluctant. I felt this vibe that she didn't want me to for some reason, but maybe I was wrong. Or maybe it was me wondering how to proceed. I couldn't bring myself to tell her about the painting of her. I didn't want her to feel self-conscious about it or feel like I had an agenda. As I painted her, I felt more of her spirit connecting with me and yet, I knew I couldn't let myself get caught up in it. To me she was like a bird. The slightest movement might cause her to fly away, and I didn't want that to happen.

CHAPTER 20

ERIN

After watching Scott drive away, I felt a flood of emotion hit me. It was like a tidal wave coming in fast to the shore. I needed to write in my journal to process it.

Friday

I was a bag of mixed emotions when Scott left tonight. On one hand, I wanted him to kiss me goodbye and at the same time I didn't. I don't want to feel like I am cheating, like Thom did to me. But then again, I am going through a divorce and the separation is legal. Is that ok? I have never even had to think through this stuff before. I just know that I don't want to lead my new life with any kind of integrity issue. But the chemistry between us was overwhelming, like a force leaning into my soul. Have I ever felt this way before? Not like this. This was something I couldn't describe. The best analogy is like an explorer on the sea looking for a sunken treasure and finding it after years of searching. It felt like I was supposed to have gone through everything in my life to find him. But this is ridiculous! I can't do this. It's too much. It's too soon. Isn't it? I mean I can't be jumping from one thing to another like this, but on the other hand who am I kidding? Thom and I were emotionally separated for years. The baby had been a hope of some kind to bring things back together.

I wish he would have invited me to Charleston. No… maybe not. That would open up an entirely new can of worms. I don't think I am ready for that yet. What am I ready for? God, what am I supposed to do? I need to call Shelia.

I closed my journal and picked up the phone.

"Hello?" She said sleepily.

"Oh my gosh, I thought it might be too late to call you. Did I wake you? I am so sorry!"

"Hey girl. That's alright. Are you OK?"

"Yeah, well… I just wanted to call." After a short pause, I blurted out. "I kissed Scott."

"What!? Wow. This is out of left field or is it?" she asked.

"We have been hanging out some. Gosh, Shelia, what am I doing? I don't even have things figured out in my life yet. This is totally not a good idea."

"Erin, stop judging yourself. Maybe it's time you start living without having your brain in control of your life all the time. Maybe it's time you let your heart have a say once in a while."

I took a deep breath and sighed "Well, it's what I am good at, right? It has worked brilliantly so far."

"Listen girl. Just Relax. You came here to discover yourself and take charge of your life, right?"

"Yeah, I did. I just wasn't expecting stuff like this to be in the picture."

"Well then, I say be like water. Go with it and see where it takes you."

"You're right." I agreed with her but with less certainty.

"And…" She paused like she wanted to insert some advice I might not like.

"And what?"

"Erin, do you believe in Jesus? In God?" she asked. I knew her tone was sincere, not critical.

"Yeah. Well… I have always felt there was a God. It seems like when I journal, I seem to talk to Him without even planning on it." I laughed, uncomfortable at the realization.

"Good. That's a start. Listen girl. I get you. A few years back right before we met, I went through a shift in my life. I am telling you. I know God brought me out of it. That's why I ask, because we haven't talked about it before; but for some reason, I wanted to tell you that."

"Really? Thanks for telling me, Shelia. I know you're looking out for me. I honestly don't know what I would do without you right now. I always wonder how you seem so relaxed. It's like things roll off of you or something; like you have this peace about you."

"There are times when life gets to me. But I do have to say that having a personal relationship with God has made all the difference in the world to me. There is a scripture about casting your cares upon Him. It's all good! I just want to be there for you. You've become like a sister I never had." The tone in her voice alluded to something bigger behind that story but I let it go.

"Hey, quick question, is that dolphin painting still for sale that I asked about?"

"Sure, but if you like it, why not ask Scott about it? I bet he'd work something out, if you buy from him personally."

"No, I don't want him to feel obligated, and it's worth a lot Shelia. I just love that dolphin. It's like she speaks to me when I look at her.

Now, I sound woo-woo. I don't know what this place is doing to me." I laughed at myself. "Anyway, thanks for talking and I will let you get some sleep."

"Love ya' girl. Call me tomorrow."

Thank God for Shelia. She had grown to be such a great friend. She was always there to listen and cheer me on without wanting anything in return. I needed to remind myself that this is what real friends are like. In all the times we had hung out, she never talked about her personal faith. I could tell that she had a peace about her and this joy behind her eyes. Now it made me wonder if there was something to it. Something I had never really understood.

"Speaking of tomorrow," she said, "I am going to a meeting at the Sea Turtle Center for the volunteers. We are gearing up for turtle season that starts in a few weeks. Since you are staying longer, maybe you could volunteer. We could use the help. After that we can go over to the Shrimp Boil and listen to some music. Just kick back, you know?"

"Sure, what time?"

"We are meeting at six o'clock to talk about it and kick the season off. Meet me at my shop and we can walk over."

"Sounds good. See you then. And Shelia?"

"Yes?"

"Thanks," I said thickly.

"Hey, that's what I am here for girl. Love ya'."

I knew Shelia's love for turtles was like mine for dolphins. It was something I wanted to learn, and it intrigued me.

As I closed my eyes on the pillow, I visualized the look Scott gave me when he kissed me. It played like a movie over and over in my head until sleep finally took over.

CHAPTER 21

ERIN

It was playing in my mind when I rolled over to see my clock at five am. I had started writing song lyrics and singing the melody in my dream. It was imprinted in my mind.

I'd ignored the pull long enough. I looked down at my tank top and shorts and didn't feel compelled to change. I had to go there. I grabbed my journal and went right to the piano. I was obsessed. Like a song playing on auto repeat, I couldn't stop the song pouring out of me. The lyrics called for me to write them down.

I sat down at the piano and began writing. I didn't want to lose the words.

When I look up in the sky
I ask myself and I wonder why
How does life keep moving on?
Like a ship upon the sea
With a tide flowing underneath
There's no knowing what may be …

I opened the piano lid and felt my hands brush the keys, sending electricity into every part of my being. My strength was putting melody to words. Before I knew it, I was composing by ear using the melody from my dream.

As the sound enveloped the room, I developed a nostalgic ache in my heart. It created a pain, yet at the same time healing me. It was as if all my bottled-up emotions were fireworks exploding from my mind and heart into my fingers.

But when I look into your eyes
All I see is you by my side
Going through this journey with me
You're in my heart you're in my soul
This I know I can't control
That's the meaning of life for me

Hours passed and before I knew it, the sun was streaming into the room with a force of its own. Hunger arose and won the fight against my heart. I got up from the piano feeling a combination of exhaustion and also excitement at feeling revitalized.

My song wasn't done yet, so I hummed the tune. The words to the second verse were lost in this deep hole that I knew would emerge in time. I wanted to honor this process, knowing it was a gift from another power.

In the shower I let the water wash over my head and body; feeling like it was soothing a deep sunburn of my soul. That was the best analogy I could think of considering that being in the sun feels amazing, yet too much leaves you tender.

These new emotions were something I couldn't describe to someone, yet they were coming out through my lyrics. Each time I would sing the verse and chorus I felt more and more alive.

I felt compelled to take my beach chair and journal to a new location on the island. I couldn't do anything except sing to myself even while I was getting dressed. I found a long print sundress and flip flops to wear.

I ate some fruit and strawberry yogurt, packed up my backpack with a couple of bottles of water, my journal and headed out. It only took about fifteen minutes to reach Driftwood Beach since it was on the far north side of the island. I parked in the lot next to the large pier where fishermen spent their days and tourists would make their way across the wooden bridge to the beach. Smooth trunks and wind-gnarled branches peeked out from the sand. The low tide exposed the soft-shaped bent wood creating a unique tapestry of ruins. Each piece had been crafted and smoothed by nature's elements.

Once I sat in my chair with my journal, the music became more prevalent in my mind. The words haunted me and put me into a trance unaware of anyone else around. The second verse began to speak.

Forget the questions of the past
Take my hand and let's not look back
For this time has come for us
Let it fuel our dreams ahead
No matter what, you'll be my friend
I just want you here with me

Cause when you look into my eyes
All I see is you by my side
Going through this journey with me
You're in my heart you're in my soul
This I know I can't control
That's the meaning of life for me

I got up from the chair to walk the beach, singing a cappella. This newly found song was now on paper and in my heart. I felt a sense of completion. It was like a new chapter coming alive from deep within me. It was feeding me, and I wanted more of this feeling. It was addictive, bringing all my senses and awareness to the surface.

Time seemed to stand still. It was like I was in my own bubble that contained new possibilities and hope that I thought I had lost so long ago. Coming out of my hypnotic state I noticed that the tide was coming in. It was already two fifteen. *Wow, how did time go by so fast?* It was time to pack up. I had plans with Shelia tonight for the volunteer meeting at the turtle center.

I put the car windows down, feeling the breeze as I drove. There was so much going on inside me. From the driver seat I looked closely at the interior of my car. It had all the bells and whistles: heated seats, Bluetooth capabilities, smooth leather everywhere. So conservative. So corporate. This car felt like it should belong to someone else. *Were you ever really a woman that matched the persona of a four-door, black Lexus sedan?* What a shift from the woman I was this morning writing that song. I liked this woman a lot better than the one that drove this car out of Charlotte.

I hoped Shelia would give me support and an ear to bend. These emotions were all rising to the surface like a wave coming ashore. After the last couple of days, I knew I needed to throw myself into something different.

CHAPTER 22

ERIN

In typical fashion I arrived ten minutes early to meet Shelia. Lateness was one of my pet peeves. Luckily, a volunteer in the turtle center gift shop let me in once I told her I was a friend of Shelia's and was here for the meeting.

"Go ahead and walk around in the museum area, honey, while you wait for your friend." the older lady smiled.

"Thanks so much."

It was hard to believe this was the very first time I was visiting the center. My other trips were spent in client meetings or out on the beach. Even though Shelia had started out as front desk help, at the turtle center several years ago, now she did mostly turtle patrol or gave night walks to tourists hoping for a chance to see a turtle nesting.

The inside of the center was truly impressive. From the ceiling hung a huge turtle skeleton replica. Around the room were education stations providing information about how turtles lay their eggs and more. Along the back wall was a huge window showing the hospital room that cared for the injured turtles.

"Hey Girlie, sorry I am late! I had to close up shop and there was one last customer who bought one of Scott's paintings!"

"Which one?" I asked, afraid of the answer.

"The turtle coming out of the ocean to lay her nest on the beach," she replied.

"Oh, I really liked that one," I said. "The moonlight reflection on the water was stunning. I am sure he will be excited over that. You know he is in Charleston at a gallery opening event this weekend."

"No, I didn't. I haven't talked to him for a while, come to think of it. I think maybe he's been preoccupied with something else," she said with a flirty look in her eyes.

I could feel my face warm with a blush.

"So, I was thinking," she said. "After this meeting tonight, let's go grab some dinner at the bistro and talk. I have a feeling that you have a lot to fill me in on. Plus, I have a little something I want to give you, but don't ask. It's a surprise!"

"Really? OK. I am already hungry so let's do that. In the meantime, what will we learn or what will I need to do tonight at this meeting?" I wondered if I was always going to sound like a business strategist in everything I did.

"Not too much. Basically, this is an orientation to see if this would be a fit for you to contribute to the cause. There is an educational session for newbies like you, but since we are together, I can tell you about it. I think it's cool that you are thinking of helping. This is all funded by private donations and it's really special. Did you know that turtles come back to the same vicinity where they hatched to lay their eggs"?

"I read about it. That is pretty amazing."

"I know, right? That is why it is so important for us to care for the turtles who come here. Every day we volunteer we create this experience for future generations. This is some of the stuff we will learn about tonight."

Just as she finished, a gentleman said "Hi everyone, I'm Dan and I will be going over some things with you tonight. Why don't we all sit over here together and get started?"

In a side room Dan gave us a PowerPoint presentation with enough turtle facts to make my head spin. "There are seven different turtle species in the world, and did you know how many of those species have been found on Jekyll? Five! The most popular is the loggerhead turtle which can weigh on average between 180 to 440 pounds. They are pretty sizable in length, too. From head to tail they can be three to four feet."

He enthusiastically continued, "What is most fascinating is that studies show after turtles hatch from the egg, the chances of them living to adulthood is only about one in four thousand. This is why we work so hard to give them the best chance to live. These little ones already have a tough road ahead of them, so we do what is considered legal to help them. Our team of biologists works from dusk to dawn making sure that if a turtle comes on shore, they are tagged with GPS tracking and are healthy. From GPS tracking we've learned that many of the adult turtles come back every year to lay their next eggs here on Jekyll. It is their home. Folks like you, the volunteers, help make this successful. Shelia here is a great example. Shelia how many years have you been a volunteer?"

"Eight years now, Dan," she said proudly.

"That's just awesome Shelia," Dan continued. "Shelia now rides turtle patrol where she works from dusk to dawn traveling the beach on our ATV to see that the nests are covered to protect them from predators like ghost crabs. In addition, she will call in any activity that the biologists need to be aware of like, a turtle coming up on shore to nest."

"So now that we have the basics down, let's check out the facility. Before we go into the hospital let's walk through the main area and look at some key stations, as well as meet a member of our family that has been with us the last three years." He walked us to a round tank where a little turtle was happily swimming, bobbing her head up above the water. "This is Daisy. Daisy was found as a sick hatchling. We brought her back here to nurse her to health and we discovered she was unable to swim properly and dive in the water. See this on the back of her shell? It is a small weight to help her develop, so that she can reenter the ocean. Our goal is to help her recover and at the same time learn how to get food so she can survive on her own. We do feedings much like a trainer would do for a dog. As silly as it sounds, we want her using her brain skills to be able to hunt for food on her own. We use this treat ball to teach her how she can get the food on her own. We are not sure if Daisy will be able to go back into the wild because she has no experience to draw from. Because she grew up here, she may not have the tools to make it. This is why we are constantly looking for volunteers to help and sponsors to support the funding to enable us to care for them."

As we watched Dan feed Daisy, I was amazed by the friendliness she showed us. She put her beak up against the tank trying to get as close to us as possible. This little turtle was adorable, and it opened my heart to see how someone could be captivated in the mission.

We continued on to the area featuring a large glass window. "This is our research and operating room," said Dan. "Our Vets and Biologists work hard to examine the turtles, take their blood and assess their conditions continuously. Let's continue around back and visit with some of the patients."

We walked into the back building that looked like a huge greenhouse with individual swimming pools for each turtle. I had never thought about how many turtles could be in one location, all with illnesses or injuries.

"How long do these turtles stay?" I asked.

"It depends. We have had turtles like Shirley who have stayed with us for a few years, yet still haven't recovered enough to survive in the wild. Shirley is now healthy, but her injury is too significant for her to function in the ocean. Luckily, we have connections throughout the country, and we work to find a home for them to live. She is going to an ocean aquarium in Wisconsin, and we are excited that she'll have a new home. It will open a spot up for another injured turtle in need."

"It's amazing, isn't it?" asked Shelia with deep pools of emotion behind her eyes.

"Yes," I said, truly amazed. "I had no idea all the work involved behind the scenes."

"Now you know why I pull all-nighters in the summertime, girl! No wonder I have no love life!" She laughed out loud.

Dan wrapped up by giving us the paperwork to start the volunteering process. Walking out with Shelia I knew that I had gotten sucked into the experience. I couldn't imagine not doing this work, if I was going to be here.

"Let's go grab some dinner. I'm starved!" I said.

"Me too! You know me, I can always eat! Just leave your car here and ride with me. I will drop you back off after."

"You sure?"

"Of course. Plus, I have something that I want to give you."

We walked in the door of the bistro and Vanessa the hostess caught Shelia up on her new apartment in Brunswick. After a quick introduction, she sat us in the back next to the large windows. The place was so comfy it felt like home.

"You have got to try the Pot Roast!" Shelia suggested. "It is mouthwatering. Oh, and I might have to get the bread pudding for dessert!"

"Well, you go on with your bad self." I laughed.

Once we ordered, she looked at me with a girlish smile, like she was about to give me a Christmas gift. "So, after our conversation last night I got to thinking and I felt like I wanted to get you something."

"What? You didn't have to do that."

"I know. I wanted to." And out of her oversized bag she pulled out a wrapped rectangular box. When I took it from her hands it felt heavy, like a dead weight.

"Should I open it now?" I asked.

"Yeah girl! That is why I brought it! Now, I know it might be a bit unconventional, but I hope you accept it, okay?"

"Shelia, you are so sweet. I am sure whatever this is I am going to love it." I said as I started unwrapping the paper at the edges trying to be as neat as possible.

The top right of the wrapper was coming off and I could tell that it was a book enclosed in some cardboard case. I peeled back a little more and in large words I saw the word LIFE and then underneath it read: New International Version of the Bible. It looked different from any other Bible I had seen before.

"Okay, before you say anything, I got this for you for a reason. This is a Bible with sections where you can write notes on the side and also has drawing areas where you can color or doodle while processing. I know it's a little artsy maybe for you, but I have one and I just love it. It allows me to read or even just chill, you know?"

"Oh, Shelia. Wow." I couldn't even remember the last time I picked up a Bible. *Wait. Yes, I do. My Dad's funeral.* It was on the podium next to where I spoke for the service. I swallowed thickly and tears came into my eyes. I didn't understand why I was getting so emotional over this gift.

"Thanks Shelia. I don't know what to say."

"Just accept it and say thanks. And… promise me you'll just enjoy it. I have some little stickies in some of the pages of verses that have helped me."

I didn't know what to say so I just stood up and hugged her right there in the middle of the place. "Oh, and I almost forgot! Here's the second part of the gift!" It was a set of colored pencils.

After I got home, I fully inspected the gift from Shelia. The beige and blue cover had swirls of fuchsia. It was beautiful. As I flipped through the pages, I came across one of the verses she had marked. It was Psalm 51:10, "Create in me a clean heart, O God, and renew a steadfast spirit within me."

It was exactly what I needed to read before peacefully falling asleep.

CHAPTER 23

SOPHIA

I couldn't believe how free I felt. I don't even know what came over me these last few days, but I had to get in the car and head towards Erin. I had this feeling that I needed to go. I always admired her drive and courage. Come hell or high water, she seemed to push through things and get things done.

Maybe that was what inspired me. As I thought about her my mind drifted to Matthew. I remember him buying this convertible six months before he got sick. "Sophia," he had said. "Let's go have some fun. Erin is all grown up with a life of her own. This is our time. Let's go to the Smokies for a few days or take a drive up the Blue Ridge Parkway together."

He was right. It had been our time, but I was too self-absorbed to see it. I was always too busy to get away. Thinking back, I realized he probably always felt that he was second place. My mind began to wander, and it made me nostalgic. I guess I was so wrapped up in work that I took time for granted. I always said, "Let's plan another week," or "I have a client that I need to work with this weekend."

Before I knew it, the window of opportunity had closed. Matthew became ill and we never did take that trip to the Smokies. We never drove with the top down along the Blue Ridge Parkway. I had lost those memories because I thought there would be time.

How in the world did I let this beautiful car sit in the garage all this time and not use it? This cherry apple red Mercedes convertible was Matthew's dream car, and it was his dream to travel. If he was watching me from up in heaven, he probably hated that I hadn't used it. Hopefully he was smiling down on me today.

That thought brought a soft smile to my lips. Even after all this time I still felt him. I still missed him. I suddenly felt very lonely.

God only had to teach me this lesson once. I didn't want to miss out on these times with Erin. Who was I kidding? I didn't want to be alone anymore. Work no longer fulfilled me the way it once had. My heart ached for something more, but I just didn't know what.

"You're right Matthew," I said out loud to him. "This is a great car." Thank you for pushing me. You are my angel, aren't you?"

As I got closer to Charleston, I got more nervous and excited at the same time. One of my clients had told me about this Bed and Breakfast that they had stayed at, and I remembered the name. I booked a couple of nights in the historic area.

Why not? Erin doesn't know I'm coming, and I need some time to decompress.

Driving across the bridge into Charleston gave me a whoosh of uncertainty and spontaneity. Even if I was by myself, I was way too young to just sit at home or work. It was time for me to rediscover myself. If I was going to focus on building my relationship with Erin, I needed to do something for myself.

Even though I went through everyday tasks and felt comfortable going to dinner alone, and with friends, it was a totally different story doing something like this. I forced myself now to go on an adventure like this. It was hard. All my earlier experiences involved Matthew. I was barely an adult when we met. It's funny how when you fall in love and become involved with another person you take on their interests and their dreams. They become a part of your own. It's hard to know where one starts, and one ends. As I thought about it my inner voice said *"What are your dreams, Sophia? What do you want to do with your life now?"*

Shoot, how did I know? I wasn't sure what I wanted to do tonight, much less the rest of my life! I do remember one time Matthew taking me to Charleston for a romantic weekend in our early years of marriage. He had never been an art enthusiast, but I loved it. I could spend hour after hour walking between the galleries looking at artwork. I loved imagining what they were thinking or feeling as they created their work. It fascinated me.

Matthew was more practical and logical minded. Sure, he was accommodating, but I always worried that he was bored with it, so most times I would not ask to do things like this. His mind also had attracted me to him. My flamboyance for life combined with his adventurous soul was a great pairing. "Like a fine wine with a fabulous appetizer!" I would always say.

Thinking back on those times brought a smile to my face yet left me contemplative. Before I knew it, I was driving through the historic area listening to my GPS give me directions to the B&B. I parked and walked into the Inn on Meeting Street. The fabulous porch and moldings filled me with admiration. Some houses back home were rich in history, but this town worked at keeping its roots. As I walked up the steps of the house, I took note of the wooden rockers and door moldings. I walked in, greeted by a lady close to my age. Taking my hand in hers, her other hand covering mine she said, "Welcome to our place. I am Anna. My husband Jim and I are your hosts." Her voice was as smooth and southern as red velvet cake. That analogy brought a smile to my face.

"Nice to meet you," I replied. "I'm Sophia. Thank you for having me." While her eyes studied me, I was able to admire them. There was warmth and kindness behind them. Her shoulder length wispy silver blond hair complimented her dark blue eyes as she released her hand from mine.

"Are you here for the Art Festival?" she asked.

"No, I didn't know about it. I am on my way to spend some time with my daughter in Georgia and I thought I would stay here for a couple of days. I have been in real estate for years and I just love the houses and architecture of this city. Where is it?"

"Here you go," she said, passing me a brochure. "The events start tonight, and they will go through the weekend. Some of the higher end galleries will have featured displays and the artist might be there as well."

"That sounds fascinating. I love art!"

"Are you alone or meeting up with anyone?"

"No, it's just me." Amazed that I was willing to share with this woman I just met only a few minutes ago. "My husband passed away a couple of years ago. We always talked about taking trips together." A few tears welled up in my eyes, but I controlled it. "So, I thought, why not now?"

'Well, then, this trip is special for you. I'll tell you what. Jim is hosting the tea tomorrow night and I was planning on going on my own. Why don't you come along? I could take you to a few of my favorite spots. There are a couple of galleries where the artist will be there." She paused for a moment, "That is, if you would like some company. It would be fun for me too."

"That would be great. Thank you so much for the offer."

"So let's plan on meeting downstairs at four-thirty and we can go get dinner and walk around," she suggested.

"Okay then." I smiled back at her.

I checked in, unpacked and looked forward to what tomorrow would bring.

CHAPTER 24

SOPHIA

The bright sunlight coming through the windows woke me up. It was only seven-fifteen, so I decided to head out for a morning walk and check out Rainbow Row and Battery Park. The walk was refreshing. I passed folks walking their dogs, taking pictures and sitting on benches people-watching. You could tell it was going to be a beautiful day. The late summer would bring the deep humidity, but this time of year was perfect. Spring decorated the houses and gardens with blooms. It was nice to stroll and take in the views. Breakfast was served from seven to ten so I headed back to the inn.

"Good morning!" Anna said with boundless energy. "Hope you're hungry! I make everything fresh so dig in!"

"Thanks Anna. I am hungry. The walk I took this morning worked up an appetite."

She was right. The spread of food was like a painted canvas. From fresh fruits to homemade biscuits with gravy, scrambled eggs and southern grits; it was impressive. Living alone didn't yield itself to me making breakfasts like this. When Erin and Thom would come to visit for the holidays, I would go all out with cooking, but it had been quite a while since they had come. *Maybe they were having problems all along and that is why she didn't come to see me.*

These were the questions that I hoped I could find answers to. It was my dream to have a closer connection to her. My mind drifted to those thoughts continuously. Once I sat down at the dining room table, other folks joined me. A mix of couples gathered around saying good morning and introducing themselves. It felt nice to hear about their reasons for coming to Charleston and their plans for the weekend. I realized from their comments that it was time for me to chime in with plans of my own, so I told them I was going shopping. I wanted to buy a new outfit for this evening.

After breakfast, everyone slowly went their own way. I freshened up and decided to do some shopping on King Street. It was something I did well. Matthew always teased me that I could be a professional shopper. I smiled to myself at that thought. The lollygag stroll through the shops led me to find a black and white flowered summer dress, strappy sandals with a wedge heel and a new bag. Wearing a new outfit gave me the courage to venture out on my own in a new place. I passed by St. Phillips Episcopal church and admired the design. My eyes were drawn to the large bolts in the building. I remember being told about how they became a standard after the 1886 earthquake.

It's amazing how something so dramatic like an earthquake can hit you and it changes everything, from the decision you make to your actions. All my life I had based my decisions around security because I had wanted more of it. But as I stared up at the building it dawned on me. *How can you have security when you can't control everything?*

Another ah-ha moment for me and a lesson I was needing to finally learn…

CHAPTER 25

SCOTT

I loved growing up near Charleston. To me, it was a step back in time and more intimate than, say, Savannah. I loved the nooks and crannies between the streets. Before getting my big boat, I would drive up for a couple of days to work and visit my parents, since they lived only a few miles up the road. Even still, I would always stay downtown so that I could meet with friends, mix in some business, and take in the feel of the city. Both sides of my family had been raised in this area, so I knew a lot of people here.

You should have asked her to come with you. That voice inside me wouldn't shut up at times. But for whatever reason, I had a feeling it wasn't the time and to be honest it was way to soon. There were too many variables to think about and I hardly knew her. For one, my parents were coming into town tomorrow for dinner and to see some of my latest painting at the gallery, after closing to the public.

Things had been rocky for a while with my dad when I left the family business. Over time, he saw that I had found happiness. Also realizing that I could make a living doing something like painting had opened his eyes. It was good to have good conversations with him like I would over design with my mom. As I got older, I had begun to understand some of the stress he might have had on his shoulders and never wanted anyone to know. He had wanted me to take over the family business and he was disappointed in me when I had stepped away from it.

My agent, Julie, wanted me to have dinner one evening with a collector who loved my work. He and his wife lived in Nashville but owned a house on Kiawah Island. He discovered my work a year ago. Since then, he wanted to meet me in hopes of hiring me for pieces specifically suited to his beach house. This would be the first time someone asked me to do something like that. Julie told me, "Scott, getting asked to do a unique project like this could take your career to another level. The art world is evolving. You could expand your brand if you would stop limiting yourself."

I was excited about this opportunity and a bit apprehensive at the same time. I was curious to find out why my work made such an impression on them. There was also some pressure to get inside of their mind and see what they liked. This project was like designing a house. I would have some idea of the architecture and the craftsmanship, but the client would share with me their insights and wish list. The collaboration would bring something totally unique to their world. I remember one time creating a refrigerated wine cellar underneath the stairs of a house that was incorporated into the dining room and seen from the spiral staircase in the foyer.

I knew that if Erin was with me, I might not be able to fully concentrate on things. I wasn't ready for her to meet my parents yet. I'd gone out for dinner with a couple of women since Amy passed away, but none brought out in me what Erin did. I didn't want to complicate things and put pressure on her to feel like she needed to do something she was not ready to do. Deep down this might be what I was feeling, and I needed to take a step back and gain some perspective.

After Amy died, I was so angry at God for what he had thrown into my life. I couldn't understand how He could put me through so much pain. My mom's faith was always so strong; passed down from my grandpa, I guess. Every day I fanned through the pages of Grandpa's writings and highlighted Bible passages. It was in those moments that I became curious to know more about how he processed his thoughts. As weird as it sounded, reading that Bible and seeing his notes was like he was sitting right there beside me helping me process my grief.

I remember stumbling upon Proverbs chapter 3 verse five where it said, "Trust in the Lord with all your heart and lean not on your own understanding." That scripture became ingrained in my mind to the point it became a part of my heart.

Thinking back on that now, I understood that Erin needed to learn this as well, and if I was going to be a representative of this scripture, I also needed to trust in how all of this with her was going to develop.

CHAPTER 26

SOPHIA

I headed down to the front porch a few minutes early to sit in the black rockers lining the width of the house. Anna stepped through the swinging front porch door, as promised, wearing a crisp magenta pink summer dress with a white crochet sweater. The white jewelry with silver accents complimented her blond hair that framed her warm, round face.

"Honey, you look beautiful", she said with a tone that would make anyone think we had been friends for twenty years.

"Thanks! You look stunning," I said as she hugged me.

"Let's head out!" She said enthusiastic.

We walked along the street for a while before Anna offered, "If you are hungry, we could stop and have an early dinner before the crowds take over."

"Sounds good to me, I didn't have much for lunch since I was shopping."

We walked into a sophisticated restaurant called the Lamplight and I could tell immediately that she had clout here. "Hi Sam!" She said in her sweet southern twang of a true Charlestonian. "This is my friend Sophia. Could you work us into my favorite seat?"

"Let me see what I can do, Ms. Anna. I will be right back." Sam replied in a deep voiced southern drawl. Within a few moments he returned. "Jorge said that if I didn't give you the seat, I would be forced to do all the dishes tonight," he joked. "Right this way."

We walked through the downstairs dining room to a stairway hidden at the back of the room and headed up. At the top of the stairs there was a large patio decorated with trees, vines, and strings of white lights. Outside heaters were sprinkled throughout the space to provide warmth in the winter and early spring. The city view was changing from dusk into the night sky, showing off the historic buildings.

"This place is beautiful," I said, as he seated us at a corner table overlooking the waterway in the distance.

"I love it here. It's like my little slice of heaven, just not as high," she said sincerely. "Jim and I discovered the restaurant and then Jorge, the owner, built this rooftop patio. We can't imagine not coming here. He and Jim have become close friends. They play golf together every week."

"Are you also friends with his wife?"

"No. I wish. I've heard she was an amazing woman. She died before we met him, and he has never remarried. At least he has this place. It's his passion, and he puts all his energy into his guests."

"That's how it has been for me with real estate, especially the last couple of years. I was able to throw myself into work and just bury my feelings after the loss of my husband, Matt. But in doing that, I cut myself off from my daughter without realizing it."

"How old is your daughter?" Anna appeared saddened by my comment.

"Erin? She'll be thirty-four in September. I can't believe how time has flown and has seemed to speed up as I have gotten older. I wonder why that happens."

I had a feeling that she could see the pain in my eyes by the way she was looking at me. Like a true friend she smiled and said, "Well honey, if it's going to speed up, we better hold on for the ride and have some fun along the way!"

"Very true," I said with a laugh. "I think you might just be the best start to this trip." Deep down I had this feeling she would be a friend for the rest of my life.

We decided to share a decadent cheese board complimented with grapes, figs, crispy breads, jams and a variety of specialty cheeses paired with salads while we enjoyed getting to know each other. She shared that she and Jim moved here eleven years after the last of their three children left for college. It had been evident that she was a southern girl and sure enough they had lived in Summerville all their lives. It was their dream to own their own bed and breakfast, so they sold their printing business and made the change.

"We love it," she said. "Sure, it requires a lot of upkeep and time, but the connection we make with people from all over the world is priceless. Plus, we love to entertain so this is the ultimate way to do it."

Instead of our waiter coming back to check on us, I saw a man coming up behind Anna heading toward our table. His elegant gait as he walked over to the table displayed great confidence. "Anna," he said with a rich European accent. "What brings you here tonight and where's Jim?" Even though he was addressing her, he looked deeply into my eyes. It felt like he was studying my every movement. It was unsettling.

"Hi Jorge! We are going to visit some of the art galleries down on Broad, especially the one where Scott Fuller will be tonight. You remember him, don't you? I talked to his mom yesterday and told her I was stopping in to see him. Forgive my manners, this is Sophia. She is staying at our place this weekend and I thought it would be fun to show her around tonight."

He took my hand in his, as if he were looking deep into my soul. "It is a pleasure to meet you, Sophia. I don't want to interrupt your conversation, just wanted to say hello this evening and offer you a complimentary glass of wine. What would you like?"

"Jorge, you know I love white wine. What about you Sophia?"

"I do, too," I answered. "Thank you so much for the offer."

"My pleasure. Is this your first time at my restaurant?"

"Yes, you have a beautiful place," I responded, trying to find something more profound to say but shaken by the way he looked at me. His warm smile lit his deep brown eyes.

As he walked away, I studied him more fully. He looked to be at least six-two with broad shoulders and long legs underneath his cashmere slacks. His full head of dark hair was sprinkled with flecks of gray on the side, adding another level of elegance and charm. No doubt he was a beautiful man, totally different in looks from Matthew's all-American dark blond, athletic physique. I couldn't remember the last time I had admired a man like this. I am not sure what brought it out of me.

Anna must have seen the look on my face studying Jorge because she looked at me with a twinkle in her eye. "He is handsome, isn't he? If you like that European sophisticated type." she joked. "I tell Jim all the time that I am surprised that he hasn't remarried in all these years. Jim says that Jorge just doesn't want to get close to anyone. He meets a woman and sees her a few times but as soon as they start connecting, he backs off for some reason. Men, I've given up trying to understand them!"

"Well, he seems happy," I said, trying to be light and not showing too much interest in the conversation.

"He is, but you can also tell when someone could be ripe to meet the right one, and he definitely fits the bill." She was quiet for a moment. "Hmm, who knows, you're both single. Maybe it's a sign."

It had been a while now since I lost Matthew, but I wasn't ready, was I? No doubt he was attractive, but admiring someone was totally different than getting involved, and I wasn't sure about opening that can of worms. Brushing off the thought I changed the subject. "So, your friend's son is an artist?"

"Yes. We watched him grow up. He used to be an architect who built custom luxury homes up till a few years ago and then he started painting. His work is breathtaking. You feel like you are inside the painting."

"I am looking forward to meeting him and seeing his work," I said.

"Alright then, let's head out."

As we walked down the stairs to the main dining room Jorge was standing at the bottom of the stairs talking with one of the wait staff. He signaled us to wait a moment. After he finished, he made his way over. "Anna it was so good to see you, and Sophia, it was a pleasure. How long are you in town?"

"I am staying through Sunday and then on to Georgia to see my daughter, but I haven't firmed up my plans yet. It's a surprise trip to see her."

"Well any friend of Anna's and Jim's is an instant friend of mine," he said with a sincere smile. "Please know that, Sophia." He took my hand and kissed the top of it gently while making eye contact. His gaze felt like he was piercing through every emotion buried in my soul. It was scary and exhilarating all at the same time. Not sure what to say, I smiled back.

"Thank you, Jorge. You have a great place here. It was nice meeting you, too."

I had this feeling that this might not be the last time I would see him.

CHAPTER 27

SCOTT

Walking into a gallery with all my art displayed still gave me mixed emotions. It was always fulfilling to see my completed works, but at the same time I felt uncomfortable during an opening. Watching someone critique or admire your work could be very unsettling, but I knew it was the best way for people to connect with my art. As I looked around, I could feel the energy. Vases of fresh green bamboo contrasted against the white walls, coupled with candles. Soft instrumental music played in the background creating a relaxed atmosphere. Hopefully that would relax me as well.

A voice broke my train of thought.

"Scott, you look great!" Julie, my agent, walked toward me. She leaned in and kissed my cheek, handing me a glass. "Here's some sparkling water. Why don't you get settled in while I begin welcoming the guests? The doors will be opening in twenty minutes."

Julie was in her late forties and had an exuberant personality. She had represented me for the last two and a half years. She discovered one of my paintings in a shop in St. Simons when I was just starting to put my work out there. Her connections really opened doors for me. I trusted her immensely and was grateful we met. Some of my friends and family were not as supportive as I needed them to be when I first began painting professionally. Julie was a breath of fresh air when I wasn't confident in my work. The only reason my art was in that St. Simon's shop back then was because a friend had prodded me to the point of annoyance, so I went along with it.

"Oh, and don't forget, we have dinner plans with the Landmarks tonight about your special project."

"I didn't forget. Mom and Dad wanted to come to the opening tonight, but they are going to meet me for dinner tomorrow instead. Would it be possible to see if the gallery could stay open for us after it closes to the public? Say seven?"

"Sure, I don't see that as a problem."

"Great. Let's do this." I found myself wringing my hands in a circular motion like I was putting on invisible lotion.

Julie's advice to relax on the sofa in the back was a good idea. Normally I would get a chance to unwind when coming up by boat, but this time I opted to spend time with Erin before I left. Even now I found myself thinking of her, those eyes and the pain behind them and the heart she had slightly opened to me. The feeling of my arms wrapped around her body made me want it again. And again. This was clearly a battle within me to drive the outcome instead of giving it to God and letting him lead things.

Trying to shift my mind off Erin and get back to work, I was eager to get to know the folks that wanted to hire me. Knowing them on a personal level would allow me to create an individualized piece suited for them. Understanding what made them want a home in the low country would help me know what they wanted to feel when they walked in the door. That was what art was supposed to do. Evoke some type of feeling in the person when their eyes gazed at the painting.

The painting of Erin was doing that to me. I couldn't believe I hadn't told her about it yet. It felt hard to read her at times. One minute she seemed like she was emotionally close to me and the next moment she was recoiling back into herself. It was hard to know how to react. I just knew I hadn't felt like this in forever. But something within me suggested she may not be ready for me. What would I do if that were the case? Wait? Hope? Grieve and move on?

I had to shake this inner conversation and get focused on tonight. I picked up my goblet of water and positioned myself in the foyer of the gallery.

One by one, people started coming in and quietly walking from painting to painting. All my work had been original up till this point, but Julie insisted that it was time to release limited editions of my work; plus, there were some big retailers interested in licensing my art. It would allow people the opportunity to enjoy my art who may not otherwise be able to afford it. It took a while to bring myself to that concept. It wasn't that I didn't want to share my work, but with so much emotion poured into my paintings it was hard to let the work be mass produced. I had an attachment to every painting I had ever done; some more than others. But she was right. It would be a shame to put that amount of work into one painting and not allow it to touch the lives of others. For whatever reason I had been given this gift after Amy's passing and I needed to honor it.

"It's showtime Scott. Are you ready to mingle?" Julie asked.

"Sure, no time like the present."

I began to wander through the crowd and introduce myself to the visitors. Questions came and answering them became natural. "How did you get your inspiration for this one?" A young woman asked. As I answered, others would gather around and listen to my thoughts and inspirations behind my work. After a few minutes I excused myself so that I could refresh my glass of water and collect my thoughts. Although I had always considered myself a social person, I had become more reserved than I remembered. Perhaps it was the contemplation or the energy I put into my work, but I had changed during this transition to painting.

As I looked around the room, I noticed two women walking through the door. They seemed excited to be here. I recognized one of my parents' friends, Anna, who used to live in Summerville before buying the bed and breakfast South of Broad. I didn't recognize the woman beside her, but something tugged at me. She seemed familiar in some way, but I couldn't figure it out. Pushing that aside, Anna and I noticed one another and immediately walked toward each other with outstretched arms.

"Oh my," she exclaimed. "Someone has all grown up on me. How did this happen so quickly?" she asked with a wink. "I just got a call that your mom and dad aren't meeting up with you until tomorrow. I was hoping to see them! It has been way too long."

"It's so good to see you Anna," I said, giving her a hug. "How is the bed and breakfast doing? I am sorry I haven't been by to visit. I feel like time has gotten away from me."

"No problem, Sugar," she said, smiling and turning her head to look around the room. "I can see that you have been a bit preoccupied." She must have realized me staring at the lady to her left and immediately said, "Forgive my manners. This is Sophia. She is staying at the bed and breakfast for a few days. I invited her to come with me tonight."

"It's a pleasure to meet you," she said.

When we shook hands, I felt a connection that I could not explain. She felt familiar. I brushed it from my mind and realized I needed to act normally. "It's wonderful to meet you. I'm Scott. Forgive my manners," I said. "Can I offer you a glass of wine or something else to drink while you walk around?"

"That would be fabulous! I would love a chardonnay if you have it." said Anna.

"Just water for me," said Sophia. "We enjoyed quite a bit of wine over dinner," she said with a laugh.

"Great. I will have Julie bring you some and let you explore. Let me know if you have any questions."

"It was very nice to meet you, Scott," said Sophia. "I am looking forward to viewing your work."

"Nice to meet you, too." I said, still perplexed about why I felt I knew this woman or had met her somewhere. Before walking away, I asked, "Have we met somewhere?"

"Not that I know of. I haven't traveled much. So, it's doubtful unless you have been to Winston-Salem, North Carolina recently."

"No, I haven't." I laughed lightly. "Well, feel free to walk around and Julie will be with you in just a few."

As I watched them peruse the gallery and study my work my mind kept coming back to Erin. Erin. In my mind. In my heart and in my soul. Already deeply embedded within.

CHAPTER 28

ERIN

The knock on the door surprised me. It was ten o'clock at night and I wasn't expecting anyone to stop by. I grabbed a sweatshirt before opening the door in my tank top with no bra. Opening the front door, I was staring into the eyes I had never wanted to see again.

"What are you doing here?" I barked, without realizing the harshness of my tone. I wanted to be anywhere from where I was at this moment.

"I had to come, Erin. I found out from Linda that you were down here. Erin, I screwed up. I don't know what to say. Please. PLEASE listen to me."

I couldn't believe this woman was standing in front of me asking me to listen to her. What did she want? Me to open the door and roll out the red carpet like I was happy to see her? I had moved on from Thom's betrayal. He was just a pansy in the situation. But her? That was another story.

"I don't think there is anything for us to say to each other. I get it. You want to get this guilt off your chest. You want to be able to rest your head on your pillow at night without thinking that you are the ultimate traitor that has ever lived, but you know what? That isn't my problem."

I got ready to slam the door in her face, but my parents raised me better than that and by God, I wasn't going to stoop to her standards. "Go back to Charlotte, Laura. Move on, live your life. Stay with Thom. Find a new friend. I am done."

She just looked at me without saying anything. This weird wall of betrayal felt as thick as the Great Wall of China between us, and I wasn't willing to tear it down.

"Erin, after all we have been through, we can't just throw away fifteen years of friendship."

"Face it, Laura, it wasn't fifteen years. You stopped being my friend God knows how long ago. The moment you acted on your emotions with Thom and choose to betray me, you made that decision."

"So that's it" She replied with this condescending tone. "You aren't even going to let me in and work this out with you. We made a pact to be friends no matter what life held."

Something hit me that I couldn't describe. I knew I had to release the pent-up anger that had formed in my last few weeks. I knew I needed to forgive her to move on in my life because that's what all the self-help books and podcasts said. That didn't mean forgetting her or not continuing as her friend. It just meant me purging the bad feelings and the resentment. I didn't want those emotions to affect this new path in my life. But I was so angry. And standing in front of her I didn't know how I was going to do it.

From the first day we met, Laura and I shared a connection that most friends would die to have. Over the college years, as roommates, we shared so many incredible times. Like during spring break when our car broke down and we had to sit on the side of the road waiting for someone to help us fix the radiator hose. We used our fake IDs to get into college bars to hear our favorite bands. We literally started out as young women and had grown up together into career women. If you would have asked me three years ago if I would ever experience this level of betrayal from her, I would have said you were crazy. Seriously. I entrusted my innermost thoughts to her. I had never told anyone things that I told her. She knew about my loss of Dad and the strain in the relationship with my mom. We shared birthdays, anniversaries and career accomplishments.

If I was going to have any chance at a new life for myself, I was going to have to do this even if I was just going through the motions of saying it and hoping at some point it would really happen.

"Laura," I sighed, "I don't know what you are expecting from me, but this is what I am willing to give. I am willing to forgive you. I am willing to walk away from this pain and from this friendship. I am willing to accept you may stay with Thom or you may not. But what I am not willing to do is keep our friendship or any kind of relationship with you. Go back home. Work on yourself. Figure out what you want in your life. Find your next chapter."

I saw the defeated look in her eyes. "I am sorry, Erin. I really messed up." She cocked her head and said softly, "You know, I will never forget you."

"Me either." It came out more sarcastic than I wanted. "Goodbye Laura." I shut the door behind me and leaned my back up against it to keep my wobbling legs from giving out from under me. My heart pounded hard up into my throat.

Then I heard the knock again. I opened the door, and she said matter of fact. "Oh, I just thought you might want to know. Thom knows where you are now."

I gently closed the door again. My stomach felt sick. I stood in disbelief, running my fingers through my hair. I felt a storm of uncertainty swirling around me. My back leaned against the closed door. I crumbled to my knees in the living room and cried.

I must have fallen asleep crying there on the floor, but something woke me. It was probably the pain that I felt, body and soul. As I lay on the floor my thoughts spun around and around. Thom was coming here? I would have to face him at some point, but my wounds were so fresh I didn't know if I could handle another round of confrontation. *How can you ever push through the pain to get to the other side?*

Although it had been just six weeks since it happened, I realized I had changed. Or maybe I was becoming more of who I already was. All these years I had pushed down what God had put me on this planet to do. Music. My songwriting and singing. How had my heart wandered so far away from my real destiny? I knew at this moment that this experience with Thom had to happen. *What if I would have continued limping along as I was?*

It wasn't too late. Someway, somehow, I was determined to fight for my destiny. To do that I had to face him; I had to face the reality of what was in front of me. But I didn't feel like I had much inside me to fight for myself.

It's happening again, isn't it? The piano beckoned to comfort me.

The melody and the words began to spill out. They felt like they were floating in my mind and with each word attached to something heavy that was putting pressure on my heart.

Oh, you hurt me, yes you did
Can't believe the things you said
How could I go on thinking we were ever friends

Now I know I must believe
that there's something real and in front of me

I gotta' hold on to this thought
I can't close my heart
I can't close my heart.

Thinking back a long time ago
We didn't know what our lives would hold
How could I have thought life would take me down this road

Now I know it's meant to be
Cause there's something real and in front of me
I'm gonna' hold on to this thought
I can't close my heart
I can't close my heart

Standin' now upon my own
feeling a strength,
a strength I've never known
how could I have never felt this way before

Now I know I can be sure
that my life holds so much more
I'm gonna' hold on to this thought
I can't close my heart
I won't close my heart

As I sat at the piano letting my feelings pour forth, I hadn't expected the amount of pain that came rushing up from my gut into my soul. It consumed me. I had pushed down the hurt so much. I had never felt so betrayed in my life. How could she have chosen him over me when I was the one that had always been by her side? I was the one who was by her side when she struggled. I was the one who was there when she needed me. Any time, at every call.

I thought by running here I could avoid my feelings, but I now realized I couldn't run anymore. As I tried to get composure, I couldn't stop the tears coming one by one steadily; a quiet river running with a strong current underneath.

I got up from the piano, walked into my bedroom and grabbed my journal and new Bible from the nightstand. The words streamed out of me onto the pages.

How did I lose myself to this point? To not see what was right in front of me all along. I knew my intuition. I knew my heart. I had known the energy when I was with her. Why didn't I want to face it and get a reality check? I know why. I had come to rely on her more than I wanted to admit. Even though I had experienced the resistance in a way I couldn't explain, I chose to ignore it. God, I was so stupid. How could I be so stupid! I don't even know what I was thinking. Shoot, I don't even know if I am thinking right now. I have never felt so betrayed in all my life. Why is my past life crumbling? Is this a sign, God? Are you telling me that I need to reinvent myself and find a way to move on?

My tears are falling like a waterfall now. I wish I could make them stop but I can't. I want this feeling to go away. I wish I had never exposed my heart so deeply to her. What was I thinking? I was thinking that I could trust her with every atom of my being.

Boy. I am a good judge of character. Maybe I need to think about what I am doing here. Am I relying on Shelia? Am I getting closer to Scott? Why? I mean really… WHY? Just to be hurt again? Sure, I've known Shelia for a long time, but I thought that Laura would never do something to hurt me. And now here is this whole other chapter of Scott. Good God, I would have to be stupid to go through this level of pain again so soon.

It is best to raise my protectors before this gets out of hand. I honestly can't trust myself right now. I hurt in every part of me so much I don't know if I will ever recover. Will I recover?

That's a really stupid question Erin. Of course, you will recover. Look at everything you have come through so far. You can't give up now even if you wanted to. Trust in yourself. Stop feeling sorry for yourself! There are tons of women that have gone through things like this. Do you honestly believe you are the only one out there? This is why you have to get over this pity party and find a way to move on from this.

Wow, I guess I am becoming my own counselor now, aren't I? Who better than me to set me straight. If it came from someone like my mother, I would detest her for telling me to stop feeling sorry for myself. Speaking of her, I wonder where she has been the last few days. So unlike her not to call and want to deep-dive into my scenario. When did I get so hateful? She is just doing what any mother would do. Why can't I realize that?

This flurry of emotion made my whole body feel numb and at the same time, exhausted. I grazed my right hand over the Bible. What could it tell me that would help this turmoil inside of me? Probably nothing. No. Maybe something. Gently I opened the pages and by some divine intervention the words popped off the page, like they were meant just for me. "Cast all your anxiety on him because he cares for you," I Peter 5:7.

Hunger wasn't even on the agenda even though I don't remember the last time I ate. Even though it was the middle of the day now I couldn't do anything but sleep if I wanted to. I changed into my ratty Duke t-shirt and crawled into bed. For a moment I could escape the perfect storm that was brewing in the background.

CHAPTER 29

SCOTT

The jingle of the bells walking into Shelia's shop always made me feel at home. "Hey there stranger!" She greeted me with her glowing smile. "Erin said you had an opening in Charleston. How did it go?"

"Pretty good, I think. The Landmarks commissioned me for 12 paintings for their beach house. So, that's kind of cool to have the freedom and creative direction. It's like being a visual storyteller, you know?" Just telling her about it was getting me more excited.

"That does sound awesome! Does that mean I might not be getting much from you for a while?"

"I'm not sure. You know how it is. Sometimes a wave of inspiration hits and I can't stop, while other times I feel like I'm blocked and can never paint again. Sometimes I don't even know where my painting comes from. It's like a channeled part of me, but I know it's the guy upstairs," I said, pointing up.

"That's for sure. I know how much your painting is like your ministry." Shelia said. "Erin said the same thing about how her music just comes out of her from nowhere."

"Her music? She hasn't mentioned that to me. When I was over at her house, she seemed very closed off about talking about music or playing the piano."

"Well, honey it sounds like you might need to have a little talk with her about that," she said, a contemplation behind her eyes, like there was something more I should be aware of.

"Have you seen her lately?" I tried to sound casual, but it was difficult. I wanted to see her. "I haven't called her since I got back yesterday. I got slammed with back-to-back phone calls and by the time I wrapped up I figured it might be too late."

"No, actually when I called a couple of days ago, she said she felt a cold coming on and was going to stay in for a few days."

"Maybe I should stop by and check on her."

"I'm sure it wouldn't hurt. When I called, she shooed me off, but I have a feeling if you show up at her door, she will have a hard time doing that to you." Shelia winked.

"Well then, that is what I'll do. And maybe she will talk to me about her music. Speaking of music, you know the people I am doing the commission work for?"

"Yeah...?"

"He is some big music guy from Nashville. Maybe I can get tickets and take her to a concert. She might like that."

"That's a great idea!" Shelia said. "That'll probably feed her inspiration. Let me know how she's feeling and tell her it's time for a girls' lunch. Would you remind her about the volunteer work at the turtle center?"

"Yes, I'll remind her."

That is exactly what I'll do… just go over there and surprise her. I sure hate to hear she might have a cold. I know that can make you feel out of sorts. But for some reason I had a feeling it was more than that. She hadn't told me too much about her past. Maybe she didn't know what to think after I kissed her. *Maybe I shouldn't have kissed her.* She was still a closed book. All she shared was just the bit about her being in the middle of a divorce. I didn't want to pry, but I also understood how pain could be masked with something else.

I pulled into her driveway. It didn't look like anyone was home, but her car was there. A beautiful day and all the curtains were drawn. That just didn't seem like her.

I knocked at the door. No answer.

Knocking louder now.

"Hello?... Erin?... Are you there?"

I saw a peek from a window curtain. "Hold on a second." she said. When she opened the door, I could see her tear-stained cheeks. She had dark circles under her eyes, yet I could detect she was trying to project a 'I'm tough. I've got this' vibe. It clearly wasn't working.

"Hey there," I said as gently as I could. I resisted the urge to not reach out and hug her, because she seemed like if I touched her, she might break into a million pieces.

She wiped the messy curls from around her face. "I'm sorry I was sleeping."

"Shelia mentioned you were fighting a cold, but I didn't realize you might be sleeping on such a beautiful day. Are you feeling ok? Can I come in?"

"Sure," she replied. "I don't think I'm contagious. Maybe it's just allergies." I could tell she was lying. But why did she need to lie to me?

"Come on in and have a seat." Her voice sounded robotic. Maybe it was the tone of defeat? Lifelessness?

There were bed pillows on the couch with a plush blanket hanging halfway off the floor. A coffee cup and a box of crackers were on the coffee table.

"Maybe we should open the curtains and let some fresh air in. It might help. How long have you been holed up in here?" I was worried about her.

"I don't know, a few days I guess." Her words seemed limp. Her eyes seemed lifeless. I had no idea what I was dealing with here. I looked into her eyes. "Erin, are you sick or is it something else? I need to know. I have to know."

"Isn't life interesting?" she asked, ignoring my question, as if she were quizzing herself and not me. "You try to go somewhere to get a footing. To get grounded. But no matter what, the issue always finds a way to follow you."

"I am not exactly sure what you are talking about, but if you mean that life has a way or circling through things you haven't totally settled in your heart, then yes, that can be true. I know I tried that when I went to my grandpa's place, after losing Amy, but a year later a whole bunch of emotions rose out of me that I thought I had put to bed. Is that what you mean?"

"I have no idea what I mean. I am too tired to even think." She collapsed her head in her hands on the couch. Quiet.

As I sat beside her, saying nothing, I realized that small, silent tears were rolling down her cheeks. Without thinking, I went over to the sliding glass doors and saw the beach backpack. I grabbed two bottles of water and a blanket. Her head was still down in between her hands so she didn't even notice what I was doing.

At that moment I knew she wouldn't fight me. I wordlessly bent down and picked her up, cradling her in my arms, with the backpack on my back.

Erin stayed quiet, nestling her head into the crook of my neck not expecting any words. "It's time to get you out of here."

It took a while and it was a workout, but I didn't care. I carried her all the way to the sandy beach. I was going to find a way to bring back a flicker of energy in those eyes. Under my breath I prayed. *"God, I don't know the pain of what Erin is going through, but please help her in some way. Give her comfort and let her know you are always with her. That you are here now."*

For the longest time we sat there on the blanket, not saying a word. Just shoulder to shoulder watching the waves roll in. It felt like a metaphor of the waves washing over her heart or at least it was what I was hoping.

I'm not sure how long time passed but she turned to me and said, "How did you know I needed this?"

"I just knew." I put my arm around her shoulders, and I played with a few strands of her hair that was draped over her shoulders. I loved how she nestled beside me. It was something I knew I would long for the rest of my life.

"Do you want to talk about it?" I had to ask even though I was hesitant to think she might.

"I guess at some point I do need to fill you in. You have been patient and shared a lot about Amy and your past. I've been a closed-up cocoon." She said in a frightened tone.

"That's ok," I said gently. "A cocoon does eventually become a butterfly." I let myself touch the end strands of her auburn hair streaked with the hints of caramel.

"That's a nice thought. I would love that freedom. I can't remember having freedom like that in forever, well, except when I write my songs."

"I stopped by to see Shelia and she told me you weren't feeling well which made me come straight over. She also mentioned that you had written a couple of songs. I had no idea that you were into that."

She laughed, with a reflective tone, "Me either. It just poured out of me. The first one came after the night you and I were on the beach."

"Really?" I asked. It was a perfect time to tell her about my painting of her, but I had to let her continue since she seemed willing to share her feelings with me. It was not the time to talk about the painting.

She continued, "The second song came while you were in Charleston. And, that one, well…" She started to close off and hug herself with a gentle rocking motion.

"Erin, tell me. What?"

"Well, you know how I said I was going through a divorce? The reason is my best friend slept with him. She was my friend for years since college. I found them together when I came home in the middle of the day to get some work papers. That is actually what brought me here. I needed to gain perspective and get away for a while. I feel like since my dad died and my miscarriage and then THIS, my whole world has been turned upside down. Every time I try to get some grounded footing something happens to topple me over. I don't know if I am making any sense of this."

I sat quietly beside her listening, respecting what she just said "Yes, I really do understand. I just wish I could tell you that it will get easier, but for whatever reason, there are things we have to work through to get to another place; the place where we are supposed to be."

"I hope you are right. I was holding on to that and then the straw broke the camel's back as they say. Laura, my friend that slept with Thom, she showed up here."

"She showed up here? How did she know where you were?" I asked.

"She's resourceful like most attorneys." she said with a sarcastic laugh. "Someone at my work told her because they don't know anything about her and Thom's affair."

"I told her that I forgive her for the betrayal. I know I have to, to move on. But I am so ANGRY with her. Shelia gave me this Bible and right before Laura showed up, I had read a passage about forgiveness. You probably know the one. Is it somewhere in Ephesians? I don't remember it exactly, but it said something like being kind to one another and forgive each other because He forgave us."

"Yes, I know that one. I memorized it because I had to come to grips with forgiving myself, even my dad for things in the past. Be kind and compassionate to one another, forgiving each other, just as in Christ, God forgave you… Ephesians 4:32."

She continued. "I know I need to forgive her, even if it is for me. I thought I forgave her but a minute later I felt like I couldn't. I go in waves of forgiveness and anger. Then forgiveness and then fear – fear that how could I have been such a terrible judge of character. And I just feel like I have lost everything that I once believed in. I have cried so much I don't even know if I have tears left in me. But just when I think I am through the other side another wave hits me. I am so exhausted."

My heart broke for her, understanding the reality of what she just told me.

"Erin," I said reassuringly, "you don't have to go through this alone. I know what I want from you and at the same time I know you must find your own way, but no matter what know I am here by your side. I don't want to push my beliefs on you, but without God I don't know how I would have made it through. I am not going to leave you, and neither is Shelia. You get that?"

"Yeah…" she seemed unconvinced.

"No…" I said with a pause, wrapping my hands gently around her face to turn her eyes toward me. "Do you get that?" She looked at me with those wet, beautiful eyes and whispered, "Yes. I do. Will you stay here tonight with me? I don't mean like, you know." she blushed. "I just don't want to be alone."

I embraced her to show her she had strength surrounding her that she couldn't find in herself.

"I wouldn't have it any other way. I can set up in the guest room."

CHAPTER 30

ERIN

After last night I felt a crack of hope pierce the darkness I was caught in. It helped having someone that understood the pain I was going through. Scott was right. I could get through all this change and come out better for it. My dad had a saying, "In the midst of struggle find the gift in it."

I thought about that a lot this morning; what was the gift hidden in these circumstances? One is I came down here to Jekyll and found refuge in a place I felt safe and with a friend I had come to love, Shelia. Another blessing was the songs I'm writing. Journaling about the pain somehow allowed me to work through things. The feeling of losing myself in the flow of my fingers gliding over the piano notes was something that I never appreciated until now. It was like an old soulmate coming back into my life, never to leave me again.

Scott had spent the entire night with me but nothing sexual happened. He confided that he was not going to be with anyone that way until he got married again— if he got married again. He shared that a lot of women he had dated didn't really understand that, considering he had been married before. I admired him for standing in his convictions. Nowadays, that seems hard to come by. He also shared how he'd gone through the grief that I was going through and how it led him to giving his life to God, fully.

I couldn't remember the last time a man just held me with no agenda. He just sat with me watching movies on the couch and eating pizza. I must have fallen asleep, because when I woke, I was laying in my bed underneath the covers wearing the same clothes.

I looked at myself and realized I was in major disrepair. My hair was a knotted mess, and my eyes were red and tired. I jumped in the shower for a quick rinse and hair wash. I put on a spaghetti strapped black dress and braided my wet hair as a quick fix.

I realized that food was finally calling my name, so I walked out to the kitchen area. I didn't see Scott around, but I felt him. His energy was here. It felt comforting. As I prepared some food, my thoughts drifted. I wish Dad could hear me play. *'He can, he is watching over you'* my little inner voice spoke back with a tone of real knowing.

"Hey, you." Scott came up from behind me while I was making coffee and circled his arms around my midsection.

"Hey yourself." I turned and hugged him. "I was wondering where you were."

"I heard you get up and start the shower, so I wanted to give you some privacy. I went outside to make some calls. I don't know what your plans are, but I was thinking we should do something to get you out of this house; just you and me."

Not sure if I felt up to facing what the real world held, I turned to face him. Looking at him energized me. His eyes shone this morning. They pulled me in.

"What are you thinking?"

"Well, your dolphins are probably calling out for you, so I think we should take my kayaks out for a while. Why don't we set up a picnic at St. Andrews? The vitamin D will do you some good too."

"That actually sounds pretty awesome," I said. "What do I need to do?"

"I have it covered. Let me run home and get the kayaks on the jeep and I will make lunch for us. Why don't you take some time for yourself and recharge? I will be back around one. Sound good?"

"That does sound pretty amazing." My anticipation started to rise thinking about the feeling of letting myself glide over the water and take in the beauty of nature. I started feeling a spark for the ocean that I hadn't felt in days.

As he walked out the door, I thought about how twenty-four hours can turn your emotions completely around. How a day can make things brighter; feel brighter; feel hopeful.

With that thought, I went over to my bed stand, picked up my journal and now my Bible too. It had become something special to me that I hadn't experienced before. I strolled to my special thinking spot, on the beach between the dunes, and the water's edge. I put down the blanket and felt the soft sand under my body. Sitting crossed-legged, I opened my journal and began.

Wednesday May 9

I forgot how amazing it could feel to have the strength of a man wrapped around my arms. For so long I had let myself forget it, because I couldn't imagine it, but now that I felt it again, I don't think I ever want to go back.

I wonder if I will keep writing songs or is this just a once-in-awhile thing? I don't know, but something has definitely been unlocked in me that I can't explain. Little words being sewn together in my head, like a tapestry that doesn't have a definitive design, while melodies dance around in my mind.

I forgot how much words and music soothed me. How they were a part of my soul. It is so wild how our lives can get so disconnected from our soul. Isn't it? Is it ambition? Is it fear? What takes us down certain paths in our careers and such? It does cause me to think. How did I turn my back on such a huge piece of my existence?

Is it when we go through a life change or a trauma that a new chapter comes up? Maybe. That is what happened with Scott. As successful as he was as an architect, look at the success he has had as an artist and that was his soul's calling. I wonder what my soul is calling me to do. I have a feeling that as I relax and allow myself, it will tell me.

In the meantime, I am hoping to see my dolphins today. If not, I just am excited about enjoying nature and being with Scott. I am brushing off these old feelings. My affirmation today is to feel like I am alive and that anything is possible.

I am holding on to that every single moment. Erin, you deserve it and can have it. Just trust your heart and all you are. Say that to yourself today on the kayak.

Shelia said I should try meditation and just being still, but I haven't done it. She said she thought it could help me process my emotions. The other day at lunch she said, "Erin, you don't realize it, but you are going through grief. You might not want to admit it, but you are." I guess I didn't want to accept that, yet the truth was, I was going through grief. It made me realize that closing a chapter in your life is like a death in some way. At the same time, I know to have a new beginning, something else has to end.

I need to stay focused on new beginnings. Even if I can just do one thing every day to keep me moving forward in some capacity, it should eventually get me to where I need to be… where I want to be.

I closed the journal and took a deep breath in. I exhaled with a windblown sound. Wow, that did feel good. How can Sheila be so right about things? Thank God for her! As much as I felt hopeful around Scott, I knew I needed to protect myself and not give one hundred percent into my feelings. There was pain to process, some fear, apprehension and probably that grief Sheila mentioned.

I opened my Bible and made a mental note to bring my colored pencils next time. I turned to Psalms because I remembered those were David's songs to God. I came upon Psalm 56:3 "When I am afraid, I put my trust in you."

I said it out loud to affirm what was being told to me. "God, I get it now. I understand what Dad was trying to show me all those years. If I turn it over to you and let you lead my life, you will take care of me. So, God, I give it all to you. You gave your Son to save me and I must give all of myself to you. So, I am. Please direct my path and help me know how I am to live. Amen."

At that moment I knew all would be ok. Somehow. Someway. It just had to be. Releasing the thought of where my life was going, I stood and shook the sand from the blanket. Walking back to the house, I actually felt a skip in my step. Today was going to be a good day. I was making it so because I decided to let Jesus live in my heart without reservation.

Promptly at one Scott knocked at the door. The look on his face reminded me of a teenager skipping school and sneaking out on an adventure for the first time. The glint in his eyes and his smile were contagious. "Ready, beautiful?" he asked, swinging his hands together into a resounding clap.

"Sure am!" I said, feeling giddy.

We took the jeep two minutes around the corner to the picnic area. "Can you take this backpack down and pick a spot? It has our snacks and some bottled water. I can manage the rest for us."

"You sure?"

"Of course. It will only take me a few minutes."

I headed down to the waters' edge. The tide was low, so we could set up on the beach and enjoy it for several hours. During high tide the beach would practically be nonexistent from St Andrews to the point. There were stories of tourists who didn't realize the beach would disappear at high tide and would get stuck. They would have to be rescued.

I found a perfect spot. Before I knew it, Scott was behind me carrying two camping chairs on his shoulder and another big bag. As he dropped them down, I saw he had brought a tailgating canopy.

"I thought some shade throughout the afternoon would be nice in between our rides," he said. In just a matter of minutes he had the two chairs strategically set up with a canopy and a small table in between for holding drinks and food.

"I'll go get the kayaks and be right back," he said excitedly.

"Let me grab mine. I want to get the hang of carrying one. It will give me practice."

"They are actually pretty light," he said. "There is an easy way to get them down to the water."

We walked back to the jeep holding hands and took them off the top. It felt good working side by side with him. Once down to our spot we laid them close to the edge of the water. "Are you ready to go out?" He asked. "I was thinking if you are up for the adventure, we would cross over into the marsh and maybe go up through the creek area."

"Is it safe to go that far?" I was concerned.

"There are some boats that come by, but they keep a watch out. We should be good to go. Plus, I want to bring my waterproof camera. The Roseate Spoonbill hangs out in the marsh, and I want to show them to you. Have you ever seen one?"

"I don't think so."

"They are like little flamingos," he said. "You will love them. Plus, dolphins love going up into the creek areas to feed and do mudding. If you haven't seen that, it is cool to watch."

"Well then, what are we waiting for?" I exclaimed, excited now. "Since you are bringing your camera, I'll bring my journal."

"Here's a Ziplock bag you can use to keep the water out," he said. "Now let's get some sunscreen on," he said. "Take off your shirt in case you want to be without it at some point." I took my shirt off exposing my bikini top. He took my shoulders and turned my back to him. As his hands touched the back of my shoulders and my upper back, I felt a surge of electricity that brought animal instinct to life. Again, this conflict arose in me, but when I let him touch me, I could feel me losing myself to it. To him. I had never thought about "religious" rules, but now in this season of my life I had become a lot more aware and actually more confused, quite honestly.

I must have gotten lost in my thoughts.

"You there, Erin?"

"Huh?" I asked.

"I said, would you mind doing my back for me, too."

"Oh, sure." I checked back into reality. "Hand it over." He passed me the lotion and turned himself around. His back was just beautiful. His skin had a golden glimmer accentuating his shoulder muscles and triceps. Little freckles speckled lightly across his upper back, giving his skin dimension, probably left over from the sun he got as a kid.

He was one beautiful man, for sure. And it was becoming clearer with each passing moment that it wasn't just his looks. His soul, and his heart had characteristics I had never seen in anyone else before.

"I put two bottles in each kayak and some more sunscreen, so we should be good to go," he said.

"OK, I am ready," I responded.

He showed me how to get in the kayak and some of the basics. I had no idea how easy it would be to maneuver. He pulled up along-side me and smiled. "So, are you ready to go? Let's turn right, toward the boat launch and bridge. As we get closer there, we will cut over."

"I will follow you," I said.

Before I knew it, we silently slipped through the water, breathing in the fresh, slightly salty air. The feel of the water cutting underneath the kayak so smoothly was exhilarating. I was hooked. I could do this every day.

I thought it would take much longer to get there, but the time flew by as we glided along together side by side.

"How about we start working our way across?" he asked.

"Sounds like a plan," I replied.

As we moved more into the middle of the sound, the water seemed smoother or maybe I was just getting more comfortable with its texture. I could tell that I was relaxed when I began humming a melody without realizing that I was even doing it. Scott couldn't hear me as he was a bit ahead of me.

The words of a song started to rise up within my soul's closet along with this melody that my spirit was creating. Luckily, we were out of the main channel and had already reached the creeks between the marsh, so I could pull out my journal. I opened to a page and wrote:

Gotta' find a way
Back to myself
Back to the dream inside of me
It's a long road, oh yes, I'm sure
But as I walk, I'll feel more pure

Like a waterfall
streaming down on me
I feel your strength holding me
I won't let go
For this I know
It is the path that I must go

"Hey, you there?" Scott's kayak slid closer to me. I was so lost in thought I hadn't even realized it.

"Oh, yeah. Sorry. A song just hit me. I think it's a song. We'll see what develops from it."

"How do the songs come to you?" he asked, resting his paddle across his lap.

"It's kind of hard to describe," I said. "It's not like I plan for a song to be written, exactly. Something just starts stirring in me and in the processing of emotions the words seem to craft themselves inside me. I don't know if that makes sense."

"I think I get it. When I sit down to paint, I have an idea in my head of what I am going to paint. Somewhere in the process it evolves into a different image then what I originally visualized. I let it flow because that's when I find that what comes out is what was supposed to be, you know?"

"Yeah, I think I do." I said with a light laugh.

We took a bend in the creek and my eyes fell upon a struggling dolphin. As I approached in my kayak, she started to make the cackling noises that we associate with a dolphin. It was like she was trying to tell me something that I would have to decipher the meaning from her actions. "Scott" I said louder to get his attention "Come take a look. I think this dolphin might be hurt, or something is definitely up."

"On my way" he said. Within a minute he glided up beside me and we stared at this dolphin, who seemed confined in some way.

"I wonder what is up with her?" I said, worried.

"I'm not sure," he said. He lifted his paddle, turning it vertical to use as a measuring indicator for the water beneath us. "It's not deep here," he said.

I couldn't figure out why that mattered until I saw what he was planning to do. I quickly realized when he put his camera in the holder of the kayak and strapped down his paddles into the bungee cords.

"Scott, you aren't getting out, are you? She is wild, you know. I don't want you to get hurt."

"Don't worry. I'll be careful" he said. "She keeps trying to tell us something. I need to get a closer look."

Before I knew it, he had taken off his shirt and was in the water going toward her.

"Ahh, I see it now," he said.

"What?"

"She has gotten herself caught in a ratty shrimp net. It is around her bottom left fin," he said with concern.

"Easy girl. We'll get this off of you."

"Look," he said. "Her belly is pink. She is expecting. Looks like she is due soon. I can feel the bulge. It's ok, sweet girl," he said so gently.

Watching her with him captivated my heart. It allowed me to see what he would be like possibly, having children of his own to raise and care for. It was like she was grateful we were there to help her.

"Erin, are you comfortable enough to get out of the kayak? I need you to swim over to mine and in the front plastic compartment next to my camera is a pocket-knife. I need that to get her free."

I was scared, but I knew it had to be done. I put the paddles away and tucked my shirt under them as well. The water had a chill, but it wasn't too bad. I knew she was getting antsy to be free from the netting. So, I got the knife and swam over to him.

"I need you to keep her calm and talk to her while I work on getting this net untangled. Can you do that?" He asked.

"Okay" I said, mesmerized by this beautiful creature. She looked to be about six feet long and bluish-gray. As I came up around her, careful to keep my hands from her mouth, I stroked her side. I could see the fear in her eyes. *God, did you bring us to her today to help her like Scott helped me yesterday?"*

Wow, I could so relate to how she was probably feeling. Yes, much better! Instinctively, I said in a soothing voice. "It's ok, sweetie, we are going to get you out of this. I promise. We aren't going to leave you." In my mind the voice came to me saying, *"And I will never leave you either, my child."* Chills came over my arms along with a feeling of intense love I had never felt in my life. Was this how God loved me? My heart and the tears in my eyes swelled at the same time.

She gave off a little squeak like she understood what I was experiencing; like she felt that Spirit too. So, I continued talking to her while Scott worked the netting that trapped her underneath the water.

"Getting tangled up doesn't feel good, does it?" I said, looking into her eyes. "I totally get it. I feel like I've had an invisible net strangling me, too," I told her, forgetting that Scott could actually hear what I was disclosing to her.

"But you know what? It's going to be ok. We're here and we are going to help you. After all pretty girl, you have a big responsibility coming up for you. I bet you can't wait to have your baby, can you? I know what that's like." I said, reminiscing about last year's loss. I knew God was healing me in a way only He could arrange. His voice spoke into my heart, *I know you lost her, but I have plans for you that you haven't seen yet. Just trust me and all of your heart will be filled. You will have another child. Let me guide you.*

This still, small inner voice that was speaking to me felt the same as when I sang. I made sure to keep talking to this sweet girl while Scott was working. "Your baby needs you and you are going to be just fine. I have faith and you need to have faith too."

As she let out deep breaths from her blowhole, I could tell that her eyes were talking to me in such a way I probably would never be able to describe to someone adequately. I felt this connection to her. I wondered if by some miracle she was my dolphin I saw the other day. Could it be?

"Did I see you the other day, pretty girl? Are you my angel?" As soon as that word escaped my lips, she uttered a crackle of confirmation. She was my dolphin. I just knew it! Was this a sign for me? That resources would come to free me from the strings that held me back?

"Almost there." Scott said. "Hold on there, girl. Be still so I don't hurt you." he said gently. A moment of silence and he said, "Got it. She's good to go."

Immediately I stepped back from her because I could tell she was ready to get moving. She knew she was free. She was ok. If she could make it, so could I.

As she swam away, we stood there in the water, captivated by what had just happened. This experience brought me to another level with Scott, and most importantly, in my faith. I knew that Jesus had orchestrated this event to show me something. We had saved her. We had shown compassion. It reminded me of the childhood stories I would hear in church about how Jesus showed compassion and healed those in need. This was such a feeling that nothing could compare to it, and it would always bond us no matter what would come from it all.

"I don't know about you, but I am ready to get back in the kayak and take a rest for a bit, how about you? He asked.

"Yeah, that is probably a good idea." I responded.

He helped me into my kayak first and I slid my tee-shirt over my head. I got my paddles back out while waiting for him to get back into his, and then we started making our way back to St. Andrews.

All of a sudden the water rippled beside me, and she appeared with a whoosh of sound blowing out her breath. "Well, hey there." I knew it was her. While talking to her I noticed a little indention in her top fin.

Hmmm… I wonder how that little scar got there.

"I'm glad you have that little nick in your fin. Now I will be able to recognize you from the others," I said smiling at her.

Who would figure that a scar could turn into something so beautiful? I felt the Spirit of God continue to speak to me. *The scars you have my child will be the most beautiful part of you, as it is in those scars that I will show you how one comes through stronger and wiser.*

She kept swimming along the right side of me acting as if she was intently listening to what I was, her eyes connecting with mine.

"Looks like you have a new friend," Scott said.

"I guess so," I said.

When we approached our picnic spot, I noticed she was still with me. "Do you mind if I don't come up right away? I think I just want to stay out here a few minutes more, if that's ok with you."

"Sure, take all the time you want. I'll get a snack ready for us." he said.

"Great. Thanks."

As he paddled toward shore, I steered to the right to make my way toward the point. I was excited to go to it. Looking to my right I noticed the pod of dolphins that she must have gotten away from. I noticed her swimming toward them. I watched the interactivity between them and how they even came up out of the water in sync, like a graceful waltz.

She swam beside two other dolphins, and they swam in unison like a choreographed dance. It was beautiful to watch. As I continued to watch she seemed to take the lead and bring the other two over to visit me. *Is that possible? Well, they do have their own way of communicating.*

"Hey there girl... Did you bring your friends? It's nice to meet y'all." I tried to keep my distance as it was a federal law. It was important to make sure that dolphins did not get used to humans so they would thrive on their own, and not rely on people for food.

But 'girl' had her own agenda. She seemed to be attracted to me, and I felt God was speaking to me through her. Being out on the water, with no one to hear me, I felt comfortable sharing my heart with her.

"Are you making sure I am ok now?" I asked sweetly. "I will be. These last few days have been tough. Who am I kidding? The last few years have been terrible. I know it will pass. Just like you, sweet girl, we all have times of struggle and times of release, don't we? I think you taught me that lesson today. Thank you."

I was talking to myself more than her. My mind went back to the melody and words that I had started right before we found her. They had been there, waiting for me.

Even when it's dark
And I can't see
You shine a light in front of me
I'm thankful for
Your guiding ways
To help me heal from this pain

Like a waterfall
Washing over me
I feel your strength holding me
It's what I know

It gives me hope
To find that love within my heart

My thoughts drifted to Scott and how he had scooped me up yesterday afternoon and carried me down to the beach. They drifted to the reading of the Bible and the conversation I had with God this morning on the beach.

Even when it's cold
And I can't sleep
I feel your warmth all over me
I know for sure
You're here for me
I'm never once wondering

Cause like a waterfall
Spilling down on me
I feel reborn
This is cleansing me
It's what I know
I have new hope
To find that love within my heart.

As I glided through the water and sang the song, with each stroke of the paddle I felt that sense of cleansing. I felt that yes, I was being reborn. This was exactly what I needed. God was showing me like never before that I had been reborn; I had been set free.

CHAPTER 31

SCOTT

Watching Erin glide along the water I couldn't help but admire the strength this woman had within. I don't know if she even knew she had it within herself to the level that I could see, but isn't that how it always is? We can't see the qualities within ourselves that we really need to see.

When she pulled up to the shore to park her kayak, I saw a glow in her I had never seen before.

"Well, it looks like you enjoyed yourself out there."

"Oh, my goodness Scott, I don't think I have ever had a day in my entire life like I had today. It's like a dream to me. I wish I could tell you what I am feeling right now."

"You don't have to, I said I can see it on your face," I said smiling. "I hope you are hungry."

"Actually, I am starving!" She exclaimed.

"Then let's eat!" I was so happy she was happy. I put out a platter of fresh fruit mixed with strawberries, blueberries, raspberries and grapes. In the dip holder was vanilla yogurt with an assortment of cheese, crackers, chutney, olives and sundried tomatoes.

"Wow, this is beautiful," she said.

"Thanks,"

Raising her water bottle she toasted. "Here's to being alive and to our sweet dolphin girl and her days ahead."

"Salute," I responded.

After a few minutes of eating in silence I couldn't wait any longer to ask. "So, I saw you writing some things down in your journal."

"Yeah," she said. "Another song came to me."

"Really?"

"Yeah, it felt good. It was like a good dose of medicine."

"Well, I can relate to that feeling. That's how I feel when I paint." I said back.

"This is so new to me, Scott. This part of me I truly think I forgot I had. Now that I am letting it come out, I can't even understand how I forgot that this was a part of who I am."

"I would love for you to sing it to me. Would you?"

"Hmm. I haven't sung for anyone in years unless you count a night of Karaoke," she laughed, "but I will if you want me to."

"Of course, I do. You've been able to see my paintings and I want to see this side of you."

"Okay. I guess there is no time like the present."

She stood up from the camping chair and inhaled a deep breath. Standing straight like a professional she began to sing. I almost had to make sure my mouth wasn't open in awe. Her voice was soothing and yet spiritual, full of emotion. It was like she was sharing her most intimate thoughts with me through her lyrics.

When she was done, I was quiet for a few minutes, before saying, "Wow, Erin. This is you. I mean I don't know what you have been doing before, but you are meant to sing and write songs. You know that, right?"

"It's happening all so fast," she said. "I mean, I know it was a part of my childhood and teen years, but this is different. It's more focused and intense than I remember. It's kind of like more purposeful or something."

"I get it. After Amy passed away, I experienced a deeper connection to art than when I was younger. It was like a part of my soul was reconstructed through painting."

"Exactly! That's how it feels to me. It's like art therapy or music therapy." She laughed.

"So, what do you think of this side of you? This is very different from the corporate advertising world you've lived in. What do you think that means?" I asked.

"I'm not sure," she answered. "I am trying not to think about it and just be in the moment, you know? Shelia keeps telling me that, so I'm really trying to take her advice."

"That sounds like good advice to me."

"Now I just have to keep practicing it," she said, coming over to ruffle my hair from behind.

Since the tide was coming back in, we packed up the canopy but left the camping chairs and backpacks out to watch the sunset. Time flew by when we were together. It was wonderful to talk to someone who understood the side where my art came from. She was on this new journey, and it was incredible to watch her gift unfold before my eyes.

I went back to the jeep and grabbed my camera bag that held my different lenses. Even after all this time, I never got tired of taking sunset photos. Each time was different and, since Amy, I guess you could say I never took another day for granted.

We sat side by side in our camping chairs, our hands intertwined taking in the view, in the quiet energy of contemplation. *I wonder if she is feeling this as strongly as I am.* I pushed the thoughts from my mind, taking Shelia's advice to be in the moment. I really needed to pray through this. I didn't feel like talking to my pastor just yet about this.

Even here with her I had an equal pull of passion. I couldn't wait to get back to my easel. I hadn't even taken her over to my house yet. I was still trying to decide when would be the right time. That would come though, and the mere thought compelled me to dive more into the beautiful soul, mind and body of this woman. That made me look at my cell phone and see the time.

In sync, her cell phone rang. "Hey, girl," she answered. I could tell by the way she responded it was Shelia. Her conversation continued and I was able to put the pieces together, even though I couldn't hear both sides.

"We had some snacks but nothing too substantial. What are you thinking? Starved actually, even though I just ate." She laughed.

I was happy to hear that, as it looked like she had lost weight over the last few weeks.

"Why don't we go down to the wharf and get something to eat?" Erin asked. "We just finished watching the sunset. I can be there in about fifteen minutes. I have a sundress in my bag and a brush to freshen up, so I don't have to go home," she said.

Man, I loved that. There was no high maintenance with her. Either she was always like that, or this little island was getting to her. She hung up the phone and turned back to me.

"Scott, would you be willing to drop me off to meet up with Shelia for dinner? You can come with me if you want."

"How 'bout you catch up, just the two of you. I want to get some work done tonight, if that's cool with you?" I responded.

I had a tug of wanting to be with her, but at the same time an urge to work on her painting. When I painted, I always felt alive but when I painted her, I felt like I was inside her soul. For some reason I still was hesitant to tell her about it. It just didn't feel like the right time. I didn't want any expectation attached to what I was working on.

Finishing up loading our things, we jumped in the jeep and got buckled up. "Thanks for the ride. Shelia will drop me back off at home afterwards."

We didn't say much as we rode along enjoying the wind in our hair with the top down. It was like there were no words needed. I reached over and took her hand as I drove, wanting to stay connected to her.

CHAPTER 32

SOPHIA

My trip to Charleston was better than I had hoped. I felt like I had found a real friend. Anna had taken me to some of the finest galleries, allowing me to mosey at my pace and take my time studying the works. I ended up extending my stay a few more days just because I could. That alone felt good. I didn't have a schedule, so I was able to surrender to the experience of finding peace. I had kept myself so busy that I often avoided the stillness where peace resides. Perhaps I was afraid; afraid of the realization that even though I was outwardly social, I was lonely. I know a big part of that loneliness was why I sought out Erin. I was hoping there was some thread of oneness that we could find together. We had both lost things in our life but the one thing we could control at this moment was making a choice to not lose each other.

I sure hope that Erin doesn't get upset with me just showing up down here. I haven't talked to her in over a week now. My fears were taking on a voice of their own. *Well, Sophia, put on that toughness you have. Don't let her push you away anymore. It's time to find a way to her heart like when she was a child. You can do it.* At least now my little voice inside was encouraging me.

In a few short hours I had turned onto the causeway leading over to Jekyll Island. The view was stunning. The long road surrounded by marsh on both sides felt like I was entering another world. I was grateful I had decided to put the top down when I had pulled off for gas in Pooler outside of Savannah. A mystical feeling enveloped me. I could feel the energy in the air as the smell of the salt air combined with the lush greens captivated me.

It was like stepping back in time before all the buildings and traffic lights were sprinkled along the beach towns nowadays.

Following the signs led me to the most beautiful hotel I could ever remember seeing. There was a rocking chair porch that lined the building and an American flag that gently blew on the top of the circular structure of the building. The trees blanketing the property were moss covered and stately, at least eighty years old. The lush green lawn and surrounding garden were well-manicured.

I pulled up to the valet under the carport, admiring the large flowers sprinkled around the entrance. "Can I help you with your bags, ma'am?" the bellman asked.

"Sure, I just need to get checked in."

"No problem," he said, smiling. "Just go up these stairs and to your right through those double doors and you can check in. I will deliver the bags to your room. What is your last name?"

"Patterson," I said.

I was anxious to get checked in. It was five-thirty, and this place was taking my breath away. No wonder Erin liked it here so much. She had told me about it right before Matthew became sick, but I was too self-absorbed to ask her more about it. When did it happen that my behavior was so unlike my true self? Had I become selfish? Was I so wrapped up in the fear of the unknown that I had forgotten to live in the present? "Yes", I said, admitting it. That was it! For whatever reason, right now in this magical setting, I realized it.

"Ma'am?" The bellman noticed I must have drifted off somewhere.

"Oh yes, sorry about that. Excuse me," I said, a little flushed.

"It's not a problem. The place is pretty, isn't it?" he asked, understandingly.

"It really is. Thank you," I said. At that moment I took the time to look at his name tag. "I appreciate it, Eric. It's very nice to meet you." I could see him light up when he heard his name. It was a lesson in that moment that I often didn't recognize people fully when it counted. This was a piece of me coming around more fully. It blew my mind that I was having to learn it at sixty-four years old.

Heading to the lobby I walked up the main stairs and noticed the white rockers adorning the porch. I could imagine people sitting there, drinking iced tea or mint juleps all those years ago. I noticed the historical plaque on the building wall. The inn was a lovely mix of luxury and history. I didn't know the details, but I looked forward to learning about its history while getting reacquainted with my daughter. And who was I kidding? I needed to get reacquainted with myself, too.

"Welcome to the Jekyll Island Club Hotel," said a young woman in her late twenties with a European accent. "How may I help you today?"

"I am checking in... Melissa," I responded. "My last name is Patterson."

"Absolutely, Ms. Patterson. I see the reservation is just for one?"

"Yes." I responded, still getting used to saying that after all this time. Still...

"Alright then. I have you in the annex part of the hotel. And you are lucky. Your room has one of the sunrooms."

She continued to inform me of the lay of the grounds as well as the spa services, breakfast, and dining options. I was impressed by the quality of services they provided for their visitors.

"If you like Ms. Patterson, we will take your bags to your room, and you can go across the way and watch the sunset from the walking path or from the rocking chairs. You don't want to miss that. I think it may end up being quite beautiful this evening."

"Well, ok then," I said gratefully with a smile. With that, she handed me a real key for the lock to my room.

Maybe I should get myself settled tonight before calling Erin tomorrow. It would give me time to think about how to let her know I was here and the purpose of my visit. Running these thoughts in my head, I didn't want to come out and say "Erin, I have been a crappy mother. Can we start over?" No, that didn't seem right. But who knows? It was the truth to me, and my heart ached at how inadequate I felt as a mom. I just hoped it wasn't too late to change what seemed laid in stone.

During my walk along the path, I couldn't stop processing all that was flowing inside me. Looking at my watch I realized I did have some time if I wanted to. *Should I call Erin? Why was I so hesitant about calling her?* I thought. My inner voice knew the answer. She had come down here to get away. Pushing the thoughts away, I proceeded to find my way to the room, meandering through the back patio terrace by a running fountain and flower laden courtyard. The place had such a peaceful feeling to it. The word that seemed to come to me was magical.

I found my room on the second floor and opened the thick white door. I walked into what would be my charming home for the next seven days and looked around. To my left was a fireplace framed with beautiful moldings. Nearby stood a chaise lounge chair and a Victorian wooden chair with a soft cushioned fabric seat. The armrests were donned in maroon upholstery with gold flowers. The king bed was stacked with pillows, and you could see the ripples of the down comforter that lay on top for extra extravagance. On the other side of the bed was the veranda. The view was stunning! It called to me to visit this special porch and spend time there. There were two white wicker rocking chairs on the old tongue and groove flooring and a side table. I went to the window and ran my hands along the molding. It was then I realized that it was a group of windows that opened like plantation shutters allowing outside air in. The breeze caused me to take a deep breath in and close my eyes for a moment. When I exhaled, I felt myself release feelings that possibly had been buried deep.

Good, I said to myself. *I was right. I do need to relax a bit before I see Erin. I want to make the right impression. The right impression? I can't believe I just said that. I mean, I birthed this girl. She was my baby. She was my soul. Exactly...* that is why it meant so much to me.

I was lost deep in thought when a knock came at the door. I opened it to see Eric, the bellman, with my bags. "Hi again, Ms. Patterson," he said with a genuine smile and a twinkle in his eye. "I have your bags for you. I don't know if anyone has mentioned the sunset in the next hour or so but keep a look out. You will be able to enjoy it from your porch."

"Thanks Eric. The front desk mentioned that there is a restaurant nearby where I can watch the sunset. Is it close? I don't feel like getting in my car after the drive."

"Sure is. It's right across the way," he responded. He walked to my porch and stretched his finger out, pointing over the building and dock across the big lawn with a crochet area benched with huge oak trees draped in thick moss.

"Perfect," I said. "I wish I had brought a camera. I can't believe how serene this place is. It's like magic."

"I know. I love it here. I was raised down the road in Waverly and we used to come here when I was little. I did summer camp at the 4-H Center and got hooked on this place. I am in college right now studying hospitality, but I would like to stay here long term. It's in my roots, you know?"

"That's so sweet, Eric. I'm glad you like what you do."

"Yes ma'am', let me know if you need anything else, alright?" His southern accent was different from Anna's velvety finish in Charleston but still sweet to hear.

"Sounds great, Eric. Thanks again." I put a tip into his hand as I shook it.

Glancing at the clock I realized I should probably head down to the outside restaurant and take in the sunset. I had no idea what was on the island, but I just wanted to relax tonight. I had plenty of time to get to know the place, and maybe Erin would do it with me. *I hoped so.*

"Maybe I should call her," I said out loud to an empty room while brushing my hair and refreshing my lipstick. *What would make me so hesitant about calling her?* My voice inside me knew the answer.

Brushing the thoughts away with one last brush stroke, I decided to walk to the restaurant. I took the stairs, taking in the stories the place held. Pictures of the early years on the island adorned the hallways. It was fascinating to see what times were like then. The back stairs led me out to the courtyard area which featured a beautiful fountain and flowers spilling over the flowerpots along the patio. I could close my eyes and think back to the time where young lovers would meet up;

children of those wealthy businessmen looking to rendezvous for the summer. Just thinking about it gave me an ache for the touch of a man. In this moment I knew I was ready for some type of companionship. The electricity in my veins when Anna's friend Jorge touched me had made me aware of that gap.

I noticed a sign that said "Gift Shop," so I thought I would breeze through for just a minute before heading down to the dock, called the Wharf. I purchased a book about the history of Jekyll that would make for perfect reading after dinner to keep me from feeling a bit lonely. Even after all this time, I got lonely. I guess I hadn't realized it back at home but being here by myself brought it to the surface.

Sophia, see what happens when you slow down, that accusing voice said inside me. *That's why you need to keep busy.* The other voice, the healing voice rose in response: *This is exactly why you are to slow down. You need to put to rest some of these emotions that aren't good for you. It's time to deal with them.* I laughed inwardly considering that even though I was sixty-four, I didn't want to recognize that.

I strolled through the shop and noticed a journal that featured a picture of a marsh painting on the cover. It was titled <u>Jekyll Island Paradise</u>. Years ago, as a teen I would write in my diary like Erin wrote when she was a teenager. How in the world had I forgotten that? The feelings of escape that came with writing just for me. *Maybe you need to do that again, Sophia. Write. Really write. About your dreams; your hopes; your loss.* Hmm. It was something to think about. I didn't even have a notebook on me, unless you counted the real estate notebook with some client information in it.

Yep, figures. Somehow those pieces of me had disintegrated like wood in a hot fire, but now it was time to stroke it with fresh flame and new wood, new stories and new relationships. That thought gave me hope. I was going to write. Why not? I didn't have anything to lose at this point, did I? *Yes, Sophia, more of yourself.* The voice of fear made me shudder.

I placed the journal and the historical book I bought in my large handbag and walked toward the riverbank. To my left was a green, three-story house decked out with marvelous front porches facing the riverfront. Across the large sprawling lawn was another house that looked like a huge dollhouse. I have no idea why, but the people that developed this island in the early 1900's called these cottages? Wow. If these "cottages" were their second home, I can't even imagine what their real houses looked like. I was curious to know more about this place. I couldn't wait to dive into my new book and read about it. I looked up and took in the majestic trees that enveloped me like a canopy. The draped moss gave the oaks a unique dimension. I bet the twisted tree trunks could tell a story all their own. Some of the branches reached high into the sky while others stretched sideways, like arms wanting to lie upon the ground to take a nap.

The stroll felt good. I breathed in the salt air as the gentle breeze relaxed me. Before I knew it, I had reached the boardwalk of the Wharf with water surrounding me. At the end I saw the tables and chairs for the outdoor dining. There was another restaurant with indoor seating, but the night and the view captivated me. A young woman with tan shorts and blue shirt, and blond hair pulled neatly in a ponytail approached me. "You can have a seat anywhere you like," she informed me. "Thank you" I responded and found a high-top table overlooking the water. I had an unobstructed view. I could already see the change of colors beginning to create a tapestry of blues, yellows and hints of peach. I reached into my bag and took out the history book about the island.

I had heard a little about the island but had no idea all the chapters of life this place held. The crisp air felt so good in my lungs. There was something in me rising that I couldn't put my finger on. Was it anticipation? It was a feeling of evolution or maybe awakening. I had read some self-help books after Matt had passed away, but I always read them with a business focus. Somehow, over time, I had allowed business to drown out a lot of the things that needed to be addressed. I trained myself to do that. Now, there was an awareness I hadn't taken the time to acknowledge what was truly within me. I realized that I was aging and at the same time I had a world of opportunity ahead. I just had to have the faith to step into it.

Sitting here with my thoughts things were becoming clearer to me. I was realizing that the relationships in my life haven't been as fulfilling as they needed to be. That is why meeting Anna in Charleston was so special. Most of my friendships had been around work. Not that there was anything wrong with that but when it came to conversations, work topics took center stage. What new listing was coming on the market; did anyone have a buyer that would be a match for it; what deal was in the works and such. Every so often there was personal chat, but it was at arms' length. Many in the office and even some competitors had come to Matthew's funeral to show their respects. There were some wonderful people in the work environment and there had been some that weren't so wonderful. There had been competitors who used my focus on Matthew's illness as a way to tell homeowners that I couldn't be as attentive to their needs. There had even been some in my own office that used that against me. I would be lying if I said it didn't hurt. They were focused on making their own living. I learned that a commission-based world was highly competitive, and some things were best not to be shared.

"Ma'am, are you ready to order?" The pretty female server broke into my daydreaming.

"The hotel said you were famous for your shrimp so I will have a half pound of the boiled shrimp and a side salad. Could I get a glass of Chardonnay, please?"

"Coming right up!" She said.

I looked down and realized through my wandering thoughts that I was still holding the book from the gift store. I opened the page.

It was incredibly fascinating to read how this island became a hunting playground for the richest men in America in the late 1800's. Millionaires and visionaries such as J.P. Morgan, Rockefeller, Vanderbilt, Pulitzer, Crane, Carnegie and Aspinwall hunted in these thick forests and relaxed on its beaches in a time called 'The Gilded Age.' The thought of all these powerhouses of knowledge, guts and creativity coming together truly blew my mind. I continued to read on and study the list of the families that made their summer homes here. These were the movers and shakers that shaped our country; from the first telephone call to the foundations of the creation of the Federal Reserve, I could imagine deals being made continuously. No wonder there had been documentation about the power of J.P. Morgan and the impression of monopolies being established. Conversations and deals were made while they played.

The pretty blonde server, Jamie, as I had come to find out from chit-chat, broke my reading and thoughts. "Here you go!" she said cheerfully. She placed a big plate of steamed shrimp in front of me and a side of red potatoes. "Thanks, Jamie." I replied. "Just let me know if you need anything else." I peeled the first shrimp and dipped it in cocktail sauce. It was to die for! No wonder the Innkeeper said they were famous for the Wild Georgia Shrimp. It was wildly delicious.

The sunset did not disappoint. It captivated me intensely. The colors of the sky evolved as the clouds and sun melded together. It went from yellow, to pink to purple and then a mixed version of those to create wisps of peach. As beautiful as this was, I couldn't get my mind off Erin. I couldn't wait anymore. Who was I kidding? I was her mother! It had been months since I had seen her, and I couldn't wait anymore. *When you get back Sophia you are going to call her.* My heart sincerely couldn't wait much longer. I was worried about how she would react to my presence here, possibly thinking I was meddling in her life. I just felt that I was supposed to be here, at this time in both of our lives.

Dusk was settling in, indicating it was time to head back. Just then I heard out of my left ear, "Mom?"

I turned to the voice I knew so well and saw her. My little girl all grown up but looking more vulnerable and more frail than I remembered. She had clearly lost weight, but I could also sense this wisdom and a maturity that I hadn't detected before.

"Hi sweetheart." Not knowing what else to say at the moment.

Her narrowing eyes staring back at me made me wonder if I had made the right decision coming here. I guess I would find out.

BOOK 2
JEKYLL POINT: THE WAY FORWARD

Erin thought she could escape her troubles by retreating to the quiet isolation of Jekyll Island, but when her estranged mother, Sophia, shows up unannounced, the sanctuary she's built begins to crumble. Sophia knows Erin is hiding something, but she has no idea what drove her daughter to this remote haven. Erin is far from happy to see her, fearing her mother's meddling will only amplify her feelings of inadequacy just as she's struggling to reclaim her identity.

In this emotionally charged reunion, Erin and Sophia are forced to confront the fractured relationship they've avoided for years. Erin, trying to piece together a life shattered by a failed marriage, must now navigate her mother's overbearing concern. Yet, hidden beneath their conflicts, a shared pain and potential for understanding lie waiting to be discovered.

Amidst the family turmoil, Erin's burgeoning relationship with Scott offers a glimmer of hope, but it's shadowed by the unresolved issues with her soon-to-be ex-husband. Erin's newfound faith in God gives her strength, but also raises more questions about her path forward. She's come so far yet feels more overwhelmed as the future begins to reveal itself. Scott, too, is wary. The reminder of his first marriage's heartbreak haunts him, and he wonders if pursuing Erin is worth the risk of being hurt again. Erin shares his fears, questioning if she can endure more pain from relationships that might only deepen her scars.

"Jekyll Point: The Way Forward" is a riveting tale of redemption, faith, and the complex bonds of love and family. As Erin contemplates whether to run away from her problems once more, readers are drawn into a gripping narrative about the struggle to find one's true self amidst life's chaos. Can Erin and her mother find common ground? Will she embrace her future with Scott, or will fear drive her back into isolation? Discover the transformative journey of a woman on the brink of self-discovery, where every decision could lead to healing or heartbreak.

Sign up for the latest updates of book announcements such as release dates, signing locations and more at www.TriciaAndreassen.com or at www.UnstoppableWarrior.com